I0544364

Thoughts on Underwear
and other essentials

Written and illustrated by
Estelle Hough

Copyright 2014 Estelle Hough

Estelle Hough

*THOUGHTS ON UNDERWEAR AND OTHER
ESSENTIALS*
Subtitle

2018

E-mail: estellehough@gmail.com

ISBN *978-0-620-62666-8*

Contents

Traveling salesladies spend time with customers and a lot of time in their car, which gives them an opportunity to contemplate the ways of the world, even if only to wonder about those customers who tell her: 'No, thank you very much. I don't wear underwear.

She can spend time expanding her own views of her product, for instance on how supportive underwear can be – not only to body parts. They are also great defense mechanisms. Oh, and they're good mood swingers... imagine...

Even older women decide to put a bit of stick in their marriages when the thought occurs. I once sold a red lace G-string to a lady who was fairly wide and over sixty. Her words to me were: 'Tonight's the night I'll shock and surprise my husband out of that armchair.'

Chapter 1: Detour to wealth

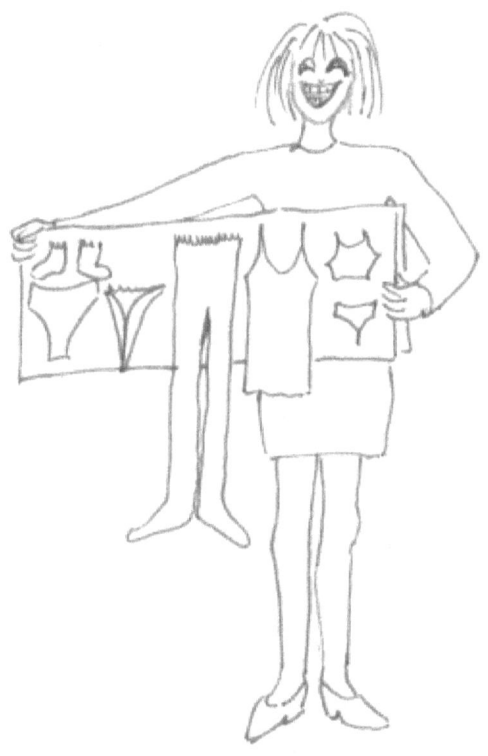

When you are young it is easy to picture yourself as an important organizer in the affairs of men. You live and love, while you work your little

backside off for someone else. But, when you reach thirty, feel for support underneath you and there is nothing, not one asset to speak of ... you begin to panic.

A few attempts at reaching for the stars and not getting there may convince you that you are one of those people who after all belong with those who have both feet firmly on the ground.

You carry on in your humble way, starting your own business. Say you become a stallholder. While your bottom gets sore from not jumping up to sell something you have 'Made yourself' and you develop either a permanent cold or your nose tan, you wonder at the viability of the: 'Make a fortune in your spare time while working from home.' advertisements.

After you have tried them and discovered that there lies the most work for the least amount of money – indeed, often you pay the advertiser – that is when you decide to start out on yet another career. (After all, the essence of commerce lies in sales.) You may then become a salesperson, or to put it bluntly, a hawker. My line happened to be undergarments.

I liked the idea, because we had just moved down to George in the Cape, where no-one knew me, the product could be hidden in a folder which does not weigh much, and I could buy direct from a factory, so in essence be my own boss.

If you live in a town like George, South Africa, it takes about 3 months at a 2 to 3 hour stretch to call on every business in town as well as the industrial area. Then you do the surrounding towns of Mossel Bay, Oudtshoorn and Knysna, including villages like Great Brak River and Sedgefield. About 10 months later you're back to George where by this time the market has changed: One or two people would have realized they like your product, some housewives would've swapped places with working women, and others will never buy from you again if you're the last vendor on earth.

George lies at the foot of the Outiniqua Mountains, about 15 kilometers from the sea. The mountains enjoy collecting clouds, so the weather isn't as fine as Mossel Bay 50 kilometers away, but the rain makes it an excellent area for vegetables, and it is almost always green.

What I enjoy about George is that you can queue at the ATM and contemplate the mountains at the same time. Although the town (city, technically) is relatively busy, there are no tall buildings – hopefully never will be.

When you come from a city like Johannesburg, the first thing you learn about a town is that it is not that easy to find work. Don't even ask what the pay is. When I arrived the salary scale could only be described as broken.

I once phoned about landscaping work. A quivery voice (I could tell he'd lived his whole life in George) answered the phone. First he described the hours; 7am till 6pm weekdays. Also Saturdays, that was from 7am – 2pm. You'd have to have a strong back, he emphasized. When I tentatively mentioned remuneration he offered a below the breadline salary, but promised that if I really knew my business, he would raise it to what a rookie in Johannesburg wouldn't have worked for part-time.

Eventually you create your own work. Unfortunately, salary structures have an effect on buying power. Luckily there are lightweight items you can carry from place to place, like underwear, which we all need. Or so I thought until I began selling it. I can't tell you how many times I've wished I could peek under the dresses of women who told me they don't wear any.

At least, basic everyday underwear doesn't cost as much as, say, an overcoat. When you use a folder or briefcase, chances are you can get past the front door of the business.

There is a moral dilemma involved with hawking. It is that employees don't like looking at stuff in their own time, while their bosses prefer that they do. As there are more employees than employers, you sell during business hours, hoping not to get caught and salving your conscience by thinking that workers will return more readily to work after a break.

Selling in your home town has the advantages of saving on time and petrol. The disadvantage is that you can never become much of a personage there – everyone knows your occupation.

Chapter 2: Styles to suit

'No thanks,' say some ladies – the smartly dressed, gold accessorized types, 'I only wear silk.' Usually, they mean anything with a slippery feel to it. There are few shops that stock pure silk underwear nowadays.

Surprisingly often you come across the opposite viewpoint. The first time it happened to me I'd been selling for about 3 months.

I was at an office where 4 women gathered around the wares. One woman became minutely interested in the underpants. After she'd stretched and turned one inside out, she asked whether it was a medium. Then she ordered a pack of 3.

'But surely Bill wears a larger size?' queried one of her friends.

'Oh, they're not for Bill, they're for me,' she said nonchalantly. 'They're much more comfortable than panties.'

Well frankly, my mouth fell open. The thought had never crossed my mind. I looked around at the other women's faces. All of them mirrored a mental picture of their friend naked, apart from wearing a pair of men's underpants. The friend, noticing the reaction, blushed, but stuck to her guns: 'Haven't you ever run short and borrowed one of your husband's?'

I was wondering about how she kept them up if her husband was larger than she, but I soon collected my thoughts as there was a sale at stake.

'Um,' I ventured, 'these don't have those special crotches sewn in, so I can imagine they'd be quite all right. And the patterns are also lovely.'

Since then women have been ordering men's tangas and men's G-strings for themselves. 'Lovely to tan in,' they say, or, 'more like a costume.' Both these styles have made to order bulges in the front. I act very blasé. 'And so much stronger,' I say.

Some women don't like a bulge at the backside, so they order their panties on the small side. And all have a gesture to describe this problem. They bring the tips of their fingers and thumb together while pulling a sour face.

Other women simply deny their size. You get this phenomenon a lot amongst younger girls. Your practiced eye may see a clear XL in front of you, but courtesy demands that you hesitate before filling in the size. At that moment she volunteers that she wears a medium. You don't want a

*disappointed client once the items arrive, so you
stress that it's a small make.*

*'Oh, but I always wear a medium,' she says
wide eyed, 'I'm sure it will be all right.'*

*You walk away wondering whether the set is
going to spend its days in a cupboard or whether
she's actually going to try and squeeze herself into
it.*

*Statistically speaking, about a third of my
ladies wore G-strings. Many of the younger brown
women loved them. They also enjoyed buying them
for their tiny tots, mostly with little matching tops.
White women are sometimes more conservative,
shrinking from the idea of children in G-strings, me
too, but it does remind one of the saying: 'Tight
arsed whiteys.'*

*The leg panty was a no-no for most colored
women, apart from the old. They associated them
with bloomers. One told me straight out: 'I
wouldn't be seen dead in that.' 'My husband will
take his blanket and go to sleep in the spare room.'
(Strangely, talking about death, some older women*

bought underwear to keep in their cupboards especially for their coffin.)

Yet sales of the leg-panty, which is almost like the lovely French knickers, but tighter around the legs, began to top those of the G-string. Some modern bathing costumes have look-alike styles. It must have been seeing them in films and TV shows, which made some women follow the trend. Even men eventually caught on, ordering more boxer shorts - or so it seemed from my perspective. Which just goes to show; it's not what you see, but how you look at it. Think of the bone through the nose!

Chapter 3: Wealth of poverty

I knew why I wasn't rich. I didn't want to do something for the whole of every day which I didn't enjoy doing in the first place, even if I did get paid for it. And easy, short work days of an enjoyable

nature for a princely wage are always hard to come by.

The problem is, one hates having to walk past all those clothing stores, (going in when you can't buy is even worse for ruining a day.) I hate going to the greengrocer and not being able to buy that jar of honey by the till, or the packet of biltong at the butcher's counter. Every time I climb into my very old car and wonder if it's going to make it I think; perhaps if I lived a less enjoyable life it wouldn't be quite so stressful.

Then I think about this colored guy who wrote about his youth. Things were good, he said, when he was young. They could afford offal most days of the week. Later on his father became ill and couldn't work. At one stage they were so poor the kids picked up discarded orange peel in the street to stay the hunger.

It makes one feel ashamed. In my youth we wouldn't stoop to offal. Of course, now it's a delicacy and I can't afford it.

Then my rich friend comes to visit and I'm

filled with envy. She has mattresses in her home that are firm, yet so light that you can bounce one on two fingers. Her husband drives the latest Land Rover; she the biggest Mercedes and they have a rare, short wheel base something just for fun. When she decides to decorate some of his offices, she gets a diamond she can put in her belly-button and dance with for payment.

If I didn't have to worry about meeting bills at the end of the month, I think the first thing I'd do would be to stop working. I'd go there and see that and be lazy and then get so-o-o bored. I'd throw my weight around, as it comes with the territory. Being the one who calls the shots, I'll forget all about the feelings of Tom, Dick and Harry - and Joe too. Then I'll begin to think that if they were half as smart as I, they wouldn't be where they were now. I wouldn't dish my money out left, right and center. I deserved it, and how would those poor sods then ever learn to stand on their own two feet? Besides, if I did, I'd end up right back where they were now, never looking good and holding my chin up. I must, if I can't take it with me, build some kind of monument. Something that will say: 'I was here.'

Stephen has two little friends whose maid sometimes accompanies them when they come to play. Sometimes we talk. She listens patiently to my moans when my rich friends go back home after a visit to their holiday home. When I've reconciled myself with my circumstances, we chat a bit.

'Why have bond rates gone up so much?' I'll complain.

'Au madam, it's terrible,' she'll say.

'Why aren't investment interest rates up accordingly?' (I don't have any investments, but my aunt has and she complains about them.)

'I don't know, madam,' she'll say, 'I don't have any savings either. I eat my salary every month.'

I found there was a beauty to the words: 'I eat my salary.' I repeated them to a Buddhist I met the following day. I walked into a shop that sells sports equipment to find her flat on the floor with her legs folded under her and her eyes closed. Anyone could have walked off with the tennis racquets. What if her boss saw her like that?

Over the lingerie I told her about what the maid had said. She said to tell the maid: 'There is nothing wrong with asking for a raise, but if the raise made her fat, she should give some of the food to those less fortunate than her. Then she would be truly happy.'

Chapter 4: Toys

Two days ago we went to the Methodist church bazaar. As usual, it was held in the Civic Center in York Street. There I bought Stephen a parachute man, a yellow yo-yo, a little plastic helicopter with attached fly-away propeller, a pack of snap cards and a tiny plastic sword. All were a bargain, considering what the ball he'd lost the day before had cost.

The attendant at the petrol station had over

inflated the ball. Stephen had hardly begun playing with his friends when a seam popped along one of the hexagonal patterns. After commiserations they took off again with the ball. Five minutes later, Stephen ran back howling. One look at the ball and I completely understood why he looked so terrified. Almost half the ball had torn across. Its innards were bulging out like human entrails, bright and shiny pink. There was no way that mass would ever go back where it belonged.

After a lengthy discussion, I convinced my son to send it to ball heaven. He'd wanted the ball to live. He couldn't stand looking at it the way it was.

It wouldn't be pierced without great effort. Stephen wanted to hang on to the outer skin. He burst into tears with each regressive step. Eventually I remembered the fête. I promised that he would get a surprise there.

Hence the parachute man and all the other second hand toys we bought there.

As the first parachute didn't last long, we

had to make new ones out of dustbin liners. It was a bit of a struggle. The thing is you have to reinforce the edges of the plastic where the string goes through with stickers, and then aim with the punch for their centers. When we eventually finished, I had to apologize to Stephen for being such an amateur.

'Don't worry Mommy,' said he, 'they're wonderful for your age.'

The parachutist was obviously not an expert jumper. First he lost one foot, then the other. But he persevered, minus his feet.

The helicopter never had its bottom half anyway – didn't need it, as it flew well without it. You took a stick from the garden, pushed it up the propeller shaft and spun the propeller as fast as you could with the other hand, then off it whirled.

Not unexpectedly, the yo-yo also caused a stir. Stephen was soon off with it to the little girl next door. She'd explained to him through the fence that her mom was a yo-yo expert. She could do the rock-a-baby, catch-the-fly and many other complicated sounding tricks. Perhaps he could learn how to do these things.

Anyway, about 10 minutes later a yellow object whizzed over the fence right across our yard. Stephen came to look for it, but couldn't find it.

'Go and look for it in our other neighbor's garden, Stephen,' I said. 'Perhaps the helicopter is also there.'

Another 10 minutes later he was back, looking most serious. Now I am going to use his words:

'Mommy, I've just had it out with Uncle Thomas.'

'Y-e-e-s?' I asked cautiously, wondering whether he had tried to take the big man on.

'I couldn't find it in uncle Thomas's garden, so I told him that if ever he saw a little yellow thing that goes up and down, sitting in his trees, he must know it's mine – Mommy, what do you call it again?'

I wonder what my neighbor is keeping his eyes open for. I'm also waiting expectantly to see what adventures will befall the snap cards and the sword.

Chapter 5: God knows

If you take the old road instead of the highway to Great Brak River, you have the mountains all the way on your right, the sea beyond the green hills on your left. Both sides have farmlands dotted with black and white cows – my mother says they're Friesians. Here and there are sheep, vegetable plantations, dams, and kingfishers, trying to catch things hiding in the dams. As the road begins to wind downwards, you

simultaneously see the sea on your left and smell the rich, rosemary-like odor of the vegetation. I think it is Buchu.

For three or four days you have marvelous time selling underwear. Most of the businesses there are smaller; the owners personally run their affairs and welcome a diversion. Generally, the shops don't have a great variety of makes on offer. George may be just around the corner, but they're still in for a drive and you still feel you're providing a service.

The first place every hawker always tries to sell at is the shoe factory, the first and only big business in town. You're drawn by the numbers who work there. Unfortunately, you can't get a shoe in the door. Understandably, they're trying to get some work done. Vendors retaliate by setting up stalls at the entrance every Friday; pay time.

When you've visited everyone you can, you leave with a satisfied feeling that half the inhabitants are now wearing your brand. You reluctantly move on to Mossel Bay.

The only feasible road to Mossel Bay is the highway. It's straight, without many distractions, so you can let your mind wander.

I see an airplane and think of my 5 year old son's worries that his father's plane will forget to stop at George and fly straight on to Cape Town. I'm tempted to tell him that his daddy drives the plane, but common sense prevails.

My son's other big question-of-the-moment is: 'How do we know God is there if we can't see Him?' At times like these you feel pleased that Mossel Bay is large enough for many drives there and back.

And many drives have not come up with a suitable answer. I know what I believe: In my youth I had to go to Sunday school like everyone else. It was a way of life, and because of that way of life it prepared a background for the time when one needs God. With that background, when you find you need Him, He is there. God can be a great comfort. But I can't tell Stephen that he should seek and then he will find - he'd certainly start looking under tables and chairs...

Perhaps a story I heard somewhere, a long time ago, will do: 'We can't see God, because He turns Himself into stardust, falling all over the world, so he can be with everyone and everything… but then again my child may insist on not bathing…

I could tell Stephen that God only shows Himself to people when he knows they're ready to see Him, so he must learn all he can to get ready. Sometimes there's nothing like bribery to start children off on a chosen path.

Chapter 6: Beating the system

People who sell undergarments do not all go about it the same way.

When I try to sell to men, they either loudly proclaim that the goods have to be modeled, (usually by someone they fancy on the staff) the ribaldry continuing until I leave without a sale – or *they smile sheepishly, say the wife buys for them and back off.*

I sell men's underpants as well; bikini briefs, tangas and G-strings too. Their wives and girlfriends buy these for them. Sometimes we have a merry time picturing the wearer.

So I was surprised when a lady I'd sold some kiddies things to, asked me whether I also sold mainly to men. Her sister, she said, sold lingerie in Johannesburg, apparently almost exclusively to men. She got them all together in an office where they bought sexy things for their wives and sweethearts.

The lady could see I was intrigued by this paragon, so she fished out a photograph of her sister. It showed a woman a little younger than I was, brown hair below the shoulders, dressed in jeans and a sloppy jersey. She wasn't the sex kitten I'd expected, yet on closer inspection it made sense – the figure was there and the rest was friendly, open and nonthreatening. I wished I could see her in action.

A woman who owned a hotel told me that she'd paid the deposit for it with money she'd made selling underwear. She'd held underwear parties. At the first party she'd get a participant to play hostess at the next party. This lady would have to invite the guests as well as convince one or two to bring snacks. For her effort she'd get a percentage to choose underwear with. The saleslady, of course, worked the percentage into her prices.

Recently, stallholders in George began selling panties and underpants. They buy inexpensive lines in bulk in Cape Town for resale at competitive prices here. If they could compete on quality as well, I'd be out of business.

Then you get ranges which look like quality, sell expensively, but don't stand up to wear and tear. We experts turn our noses up at them. We think of it as cheating.

Yet it's so easy to cheat ourselves. Just yesterday I charged someone full price for something I'd gotten at half. With my ill-gotten gains I bought a warm, flaky chicken pie.

It started me off thinking and soon I imagined what it would be like being a fully-fledged, successful crook, one thing leading to another. My only worries would be that I may get caught, and that my children would hear about my nefarious dealings and would be ashamed of me.

But, say I'm lucky, I die a rich crook with only an ulcer to show for it. (After all there may be some worries about getting done in by people I have done out.) My children inherit. But now they are involved and some of our community admired my success so much they thought it was OK to become crooks and the first thing they stole was some of my daughter's ill-gotten gains, as she was the easiest target and she hadn't earned it anyway.

More places go bankrupt to fill crooks pockets. The country's honest people become poorer and more dissatisfied with their lot in life, some of them turning to crime. By now my children have to pay through the nose for what they buy, to make up for losses through crime. Someone shoots my son for his car.

Did I really beat the system?

I decide to curb my inclinations towards crookery. From now on I shall take note of the ripples caused by the stones I throw in the pond, I think as I brush pastry flakes off my lap.

Chapter 7: Superman

Until recently my son was an avid Superman fan. His enthusiasm cooled somewhat when Lois and Clark, in the latest TV version, began making preparations for their wedding. (Stephen was mainly interested in watching Superman fly with his cape billowing out behind him, and lifting *trucks up with one hand.)*

During the wedding night episode, when the fake Lois ate a couple of frogs with relish, Stephen suddenly wandered out. So far he hasn't bothered to watch again.

To him it must have been a big letdown, seeing hero material turn into soppy horror. Before this, all he wanted for Christmas was a Superman outfit. All day long he walked around with a towel cape pinned to the neckbands of his T-shirts. He practiced by climbing up the gate and jumping off the front wall. Whenever he ate a lollipop, he'd untwist the front end of the wrapper, pull it straight back and fly the sucker, calling: 'Superm-a-a-a-n comes to the rescue!'

Stephen loves a good boxing match with his mother, even though I'm a bit of a sissy. The problem is the child doesn't hold back. So, one night when he insisted on fighting with me on my bed, I suggested that we didn't box with our fists. We were tiny mice, so we could only box with crooked forefingers.

As usual, the game became heated. Pow-pow-pow. It became surprisingly tiring, so we had proper rounds and count-downs. Stephen's mouse got the upper hand. With a mighty blow on my knuckle his mouse flew up into the air. Excitedly he shouted: 'Superm-o-u-s-e!'

From then on he couldn't be stopped. Everything good was a flying super hero. When he ate a cookie it would suddenly fly through the air and be a Super Coo-oo-kie!

Another day proved that I wasn't such a sissy after all. We have two large Silky Oaks growing next to the house. The wind continuously blows leaves onto our flat roof. Luckily the flatness of the roof makes it easy to clear the leaves out of the gutters. The only problem this time was that a Superman crazy child with a towel hanging from his neck kept on following me up the ladder. And he wouldn't listen. Five minutes after the reprimand he'd be trying the same thing again.

After I'd warned him off the roof for the umpteenth time - I was what they call thoroughly vexed – I pulled the ladder up after me. Stephen stood there watching, but instead of bursting into tears like I expected him to, my superhuman strength must have impressed him. He made muscles with his arms, shouting: 'Superm-o-o-m!

That was when I decided that he could have a Superman outfit for Christmas. But with the frog eating Superman fiasco, what on earth am I going to get him now?

Chapter 8: Bribery and corruption

The dog had to go to the vet., which meant I couldn't go to Mossel Bay and be back in time to pick Stephen up at the crèche. So I decided to sell in George's industrial area. There's a horse-shoe shaped street tucked away in such a way that you wouldn't know it existed if you weren't looking for an address there on the street map. This street

needed some of my attention.

But before I get to one of my calls there, let me tell you about a television program I watched a few months ago, which has some relevance to the story. It was called: 'Zaire – a country gone to seed.'

Ecologically one of the richest countries in the world, it is being raped, concerned people say, through mismanagement. Scene after scene was shown of its rainforests being chopped down. The continuously increasing population burn more and more of the natural vegetation to plant crops. Its wild animals are captured for food and the tourist pet trade. Everything is edible, nothing sacred. Animals are tied in inhumane ways to restrict movement, but to keep the meat fresh. 90% of Kinshasa, the capital, is a slum, they say. Corruption is a way of life for most. Yet there is still the odd inhabitant who stands up for what are right and good. For instance, a school teacher who is owed 10 months' salary by the government continues to teach. Children have to learn, he says. Others form private societies for their own improvement. They pool their resources for

*projects they're interested in as the banks have
failed.*

*The photographer in the program films
scenes where they are, time and again, accosted by
officials demanding bribe money. If they don't
oblige, their equipment will be confiscated, despite
their having every conceivable permit on hand.*

*In a dilapidated hospital there is literally
nothing besides a 10 year old supply of one
particular drug – no beds, no blankets, no food, no
nurses, only the doctor. He says people stay at
home when they get sick; why die there?*

*While calling at a concrete manufacturer,
when I was selling in this horse-shoe street I was
talking about, I was reminded of the program on
Zaire.*

*The man behind the counter laughed. He
said he didn't have a receptionist at the moment
who may be interested in lingerie. We started
chatting. I was interested in a particular hollow
brick I'd seen on display at the George Show
Grounds. He told me that he'd stopped production*

on this brick. I was disappointed, as it was the ideal thing for quick, economical building if you're a DIY person. The bricks fitted into each other, so you didn't need cement. Even plastering was only a thick paint wash, which ended up looking exactly like a plastered wall. And it was durable.

I needed a garage, so I asked him why.

He answered: 'As a new product on the market it needed consumer confidence, you know, lots of people seeing it being used to good effect. I was offered just the thing, a municipal contract. With the new government being big on houses for lower income groups, it could launch the product.

Unfortunately certain council members suggested that on the first 200 houses they awarded me I should give them 20 cents a brick back 'under the table' so to speak. I knew that if I complied I'd sit with a bad conscience, plus be vulnerable to exposure, and they'd be getting away with theft. So I told them to stuff their contract. Unfortunately, without such a big contract it's difficult to make the brick visible. It's only viable on a bigger scale.'

I told the man the story about Zaire and what a good thing it was he stood fast.

By the time I got out of there, I realized there was no more time left for selling, if I were to be on time to pick up Stephen.

Chapter 9: Souls forever

    Today I had an argument with a female steamroller about religion. Why it happened over my panty display I don't know – oh yes, I see the connection; Adam and Eve being sent out naked from paradise.

She was disgusted with the lacy G-strings; evil, she called them, so as we were on the subject I said that it got my goat how preachers harped on naked Eve being seduced by the snake. Now everyone thinks that sex and snakes are the issue. They don't even realize the story is about becoming aware of good and bad. Knowledge is the culprit – not sex!

She said it was all very good and well, but snakes were evil, because God punished them for getting ideas above their heads by making them sail on their bellies. I just sighed; here she was confusing the devil with snakes. Also, she said, Adam and Eve were suddenly ashamed of being naked; therefore sex was very much the issue. She went on to say that even today when sex got the upper hand over common sense it was evil. That reminded me of a few situations in my past where control was not the issue, but I wisely kept my mouth shut – she was busy stretching the XL full briefs to test the extra strong elastic.

It's also very good and well, I thought while driving home, but I've got many more points to make. So, when I got home I continued the *argument with my mother.*

We went through the tree of knowledge to the tree of eternal life while I had my cheese and tomato sandwiches and tea.

Mom believes when you're dead you're dead – there's nothing but the full stop. Speaking for myself, for an embarrassingly long time I thought that living eternally had something to do with a pill being discovered that would keep our bodies intact forever. One day the light dawned: We were made in the image of God who did not need a body at all, except that our souls were not as yet holy.

I thought that it was time my mother woke up to this spirit thing, so I told her about a true story I'd read:

A doctor sits by a dying patient's bed. It looks like she drifts off. When she wakes up she tells him that she'd just left her body. She floated up, out of the ward, down the corridor to another ward on another floor. There she saw a patient sitting up in her bed, wearing a bed jacket and writing a letter. She floated to her and read the letter over her shoulder.

The doctor asks her to describe the other patient and where she's lying. He also asks what she's written. Then he goes to check up.

He finds the other patient in her bed-jacket and after explanations sees that the contents of the letter are as stated. The old lady who had the out of body experience dies an hour or two later.

'So, mother dear, how do you explain it?' I asked.

'I don't know,' said Mom, 'perhaps the brain sends out strong electrical impulses during times of stress, like death, that pick things up.'

So I said: 'It doesn't matter whether you call them electrical impulses or your soul, her experiences were in the corridor and in the other ward, while her body remained in bed.'

'If the story is true,' said my infuriating mother,' how do we know that the electrical impulses persist after the death of the body?'

'Ghosts!' I shouted. 'There are millions of ghost stories floating around.'

(OK, I know ghosts are supposed to be earthbound and spirits up there, but they both float.)

'How can you verify them?' asked my mother, forever calm, 'I've never seen one.'

I wanted to blow a gasket. But your son has, I wanted to say, but then I realized that she'd only say he might have been mistaken. After all, we believe what we want to believe.

My headache still hadn't cleared up. It just showed you, I thought, what trouble Eve had brought down on our heads by teaching us to think. Perhaps we should do something about that tree of eternal life – like hide it somewhere.

Chapter 10: Beauty

As a teenager, my cousin Linda used to hide away in her cupboard from all the boyfriends she didn't want. I was the one who had to make the excuses for her.

I see things haven't changed. Recently, she

and her son came for a visit. We were crossing the street to explore the neighborhood when a motorist stopped to ask the way somewhere. He looked intently into Linda's wonderfully shaped grey eyes. She explained that she didn't know the area. He thanked her with a broad smile and drove off. He would've driven over my foot if I hadn't yanked it away in time. And I know exactly where the street is he was looking for!

Not long afterwards, my other beautiful friend, Annatjie, came to visit. Two doors from me the neighbours had contracted someone to fell their trees. Annatjie asked the contractor in passing what he was going to do with all the wood. Within minutes her 4x4 was piled high with fireplace size sawn off logs.

The following morning I got a flat tyre coming out of my driveway. The contractor was in his pickup reading the newspaper. When he noticed me getting a tyre out of my boot, he started it quickly. 'Sorry,' he called out in passing, 'I'm in a great hurry this morning!'

It is at times like these that I sit down, take

my shoes off and admire my hidden beauty – my feet.

In America they once experimented with children of six and seven. For six months at a time they dressed these kids badly and accessorized with braces, dowdy hairstyles and specs. The same children, who for the next six months wore ringlets, were minus specs and wore high fashion clothing, got much better marks at their new school.

Look at older people. A lot is said about inner beauty, the value of earned wrinkles and so forth. Having a facelift is regarded as a superficial act. Perhaps, when you're associating with those who know your innermost soul... but even they enjoy looking at pleasing things. It's as if people have to gear themselves up, before they can appreciate intrinsic value above beauty. And let's face it; humans don't like making the effort. It's easier to see the inner glow on a self-confident, well cared for older face, than on a broken-spirited uncared for one.

I noticed that naturally attractive people mostly strived to look good, so I thought that if I strived too, perhaps I could fool some people into thinking I was also good looking. My son noticed my efforts. The other day he was watching me carefully as I applied face cream. He even made space for himself on the dressing-table.

'Why do you put that stuff on?' He asked.

'My face feels dry and I'm worried about getting wrinkles.' I answered.

He took my face in both his little hands and crooned: 'But you're so beautiful. Look at all those little red dots (broken veins) on your cheeks. They're just like tiny mouse tracks all over your face.'

And it is at times like these that I believe that beauty can be found where love is.

Chapter 11: Appearances

It was one of those awful days.

My green Mazda 323 has seen better days, but yesterday I thought my clothes inspired more confidence. I stepped out of the car in Mossel Bay, hugging my folder. There was a woman doing what looked like administrative work, in a glass enclosure in a hardware store and I was aiming for her.

Out of the corner of my eye I saw someone stepping across to block my way. I'd noticed this man looking me up and down as I locked the car, but had taken him for a customer at the store eyeing me, even if in a dubious way.

He asked me what my business was. I told him. He said he couldn't allow it. (By now I realized that he was the owner of the store.) I said I understood and walked out. No attitude – politely. I think I even smiled.

The crunch came when he followed me out. He told me to move my car as the parking was meant for customers. There was no sign up and my car was the only one in the six available spaces in front of his shop.

My ego was crushed. Who could have a sprightly demeanor after that? I drove to Mossel Bay point to watch the sea for a while.

The point has rocky ledges around which the sea plays. To the right the ground rises steeply to a large hollowed out cave. Dassies sun themselves on the ridges rising to the cave. It's marvelously calming to sit there.

If I met one more person who thought they could walk all over me, because I was a hawker, I thought, I'd give up my job. Why did some people treat those who they imagined to be below them on the social scale with contempt? What did they know about them after all?

I entertained myself thinking that 150 years ago I would have been demeaned for trying to earn a living. I would be frowned upon even for sitting alone, unescorted, and for trying to get my face and legs tanned.

Nowadays, one of the ultimate status symbols would be to have the title: 'Dr.' in front of your name, but 150 years ago, you'd have been looked down upon for that.

All these attitudes, fashions, were nothing but the desire to seem superior, to impress your status on those around you. It makes you feel acceptable, and hopefully sought after by your peers. Why was it, I thought, that our egos are so fragile that what we appear to be to each other is so important; how we dress, what our cars look like, our intelligence and talents, who we're married to or at which places we are seen? We aim for the highest possible pinnacles, and so often our measures are affluence, apparent or real. We forget, or simply don't measure that far – that the highest pinnacles ever reached were in situations where money might have been the ruination of success (Van Gogh) or was not relevant (Mahatma Gandhi, Mother Theresa) or was eschewed (Jesus).

Thinking along these lines made me feel much better. It did not make me feel like returning to work though, so I declared the rest of the day a holiday.

Chapter 12: 'Reality'

Let's go back in history to before the continents shifted, to before the first single-cell life form made its mark, to where the earth was formed from floating debris, particles being attracted to each other until they formed a more or less solid mass.

What the heck, let's shoot right back to where there was nothing. Nothing to this side, nothing to that side, nothing all around for such a long time that you'd think it should get dusty. But that would be jumping the gun. I think nothing was around for so long that it got bored and built up some latent energy.

Somewhere in almost nothing some of this energy must've become attracted to some other energy, while rejecting other. What is awareness without love and hate after all? Through eons (who's looking at time?) protons and neutrons formed electrical charges; electromagnetism. Movement had been created. Particles had formed. Molecules built up. In other words, nothing became dusty. Dust cohered, turning into worlds. Nothing became something.

Now you may wonder where all this is leading to. I'll tell you. The other day I was watching television. Physicists at the quantum physics laboratory in Switzerland were discussing a tubular track they have there. Apparently they send particles along this track at a speed faster than the speed of light – faster than 186,000 miles per second. They photograph these moving particles with an impressive camera. (It's huge). At a very great speed, they've managed to capture the change of particles from particle to pure energy. In loose terms; they've managed to turn something back into almost nothing, as far as we can see. Matter vibrating greatly becomes non-matter.

With a great leap of the imagination you can suddenly see physicists and metaphysicists on speaking terms. Or perhaps scientists have long ago dropped their stance about observable data. Anyway, it brings us a step closer to understanding about poltergeists, ghosts, strange disappearances and appearances of spaceships or what-not... There must be a link if particles and energy can transform with the right vibrations. And, oh yes, they've discovered that particles/waves choose their own paths when they come to places where there is an option – it seems they are intelligent too. Ha!

On top of all the observable data we have gathered, it is beginning to appear that what we've always regarded as most suspiciously spooky can be done and is actually natural, or at most a *deviant path of nature, but not Supernatural anymore – simply not yet fully understood. Isn't it weird to think that our understanding of what is, is not necessarily reality at all?*

Now we see it, now we don't, it all began as energy and that is what it still is, just seemingly transformed with progression.

Now, if you've noticed that I haven't actually come to a point yet, you're right, I haven't. I'm simply sprouting my theory about life, because I find it fascinating. You may call it my half-baked theory if you like.

Chapter 13: Pizza and cookies

Today it happened again. Mom put milk in

Stephen's porridge. For the past six months he's asked her every time we have mealy meal not to put milk in it. He prefers a dollop of butter. She says milk is good for him. He says he'll have it separately in a glass. She ignores this for a not communicated reason.

Mom does almost all the cooking. When I get the urge to cook, she's an uninvited overseer until my creation is her creation. For me it's best to lock the kitchen door and not go to the toilet while cooking.

Mom is good at everything from roasts, to veggies, to soup, but don't ask for something as outlandish as Italian. You'll get watery spaghetti and no garlic. This is the only area where I've made an inroad. What I find strange is that we never get watery macaroni and cheese. It must be a totally Anglicized dish.

The herbs and spices my mother identifies with, apart from parsley, are cloves, nutmeg, cinnamon and the occasional bay leaf. I think in terms of parsley, sage, thyme, celery and garlic.

She starts the meat at 2pm. for 5. Unless it's a special occasion, I wouldn't dream of standing in front of the stove for more than half an hour. I'd also like to eat later.

It's useless to try and change her. I've tried. At first she'll take no notice, confident that her way is the best. However, she does not like her children to suffer. When I've nagged myself into unhappiness, she notices and becomes distressed. For once, just to please me, she'll do whatever it is, my way. Tomorrow all will be forgotten and she'll continue as usual.

Mom gets upset if someone wants to organize an outing on a Monday or a Tuesday. Monday is wash day and Tuesday for ironing. Only rain is allowed to change that.

(In case you're getting the idea that yours truly does absolutely nothing, this is only half true. In my defense and so you'd understand that there is harmony in our household, I clean and garden as little as possible.)

Mom likes to go visiting at fixed times. She

may, for instance, get restless at 4pm. on a Sunday afternoon.

She definitely does not enjoy sleeping in any other bed than her own. The only times she'll force herself to is when she could thereby see more of one or the other of her sons.

Talk about inflexible! But according to psychologists, there go you and I at seventy-something. They have it all mapped out: at 15 you think you know everything, at 18 you fight the establishment, at 23 you think of nest building, at 29 you have an affair, at 40 your views on life change, etc.

It's true. All my friends at just past 40 began saying things like: Money doesn't mean that much to me anymore. They begin to be more considerate of others, get urges to do something for charity... In their 50's they'll most probably do it... or decide to travel.

So we all look different and have different backgrounds. Once we understand that we're actually all little clones we may rub along quite *famously.*

That's why Mom and I don't waste our breath fighting anymore. She knows I have a lot to learn and I know her brain's petrified. One has to make allowances for these things. Stephen is also tolerably happy; he gets pizza from one and cookies from the other.

Chapter 14: Dream travel

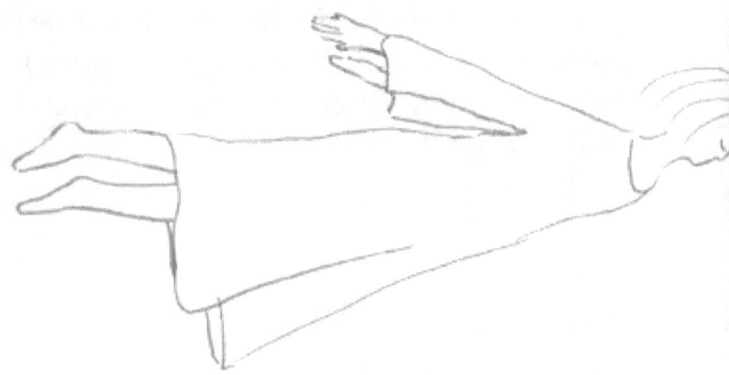

As a young woman, my aunt had a dashing pilot for a husband. She was still in love and naturally anxious when he had to fight for England during the Second World War.

One night she dreamt she saw his plane going down over the sea. The next moment in the dream she was in a shop buying mourning clothes. The assistant was asking her whether she'd require black stockings as well. With tears in her eyes she answered: 'No, thank you. That would be *overdoing the black.'*

A week or two later she was informed that her husband's aero plane had been shot down over the Indian Ocean. She was devastated but prepared for the funeral.

A few days later she was standing in a shop buying black gloves and a dress. The assistant asked: 'Does Madam require black stockings as well?' The tears welled up in her eyes as she answered with the same words as in the dream. Recognition of the duplication came when she realized that the shop assistant's face was the same as the one in the dream – a woman she'd never otherwise seen before.

Some people have precognitive dreams, others don't, as far as they can recall, and probably ascribe them to deja vue.

As a teenager I had a few vivid ones, so I know they exist. These happened during a turbulent period in our household. People who've studied the phenomenon say that these are exactly the times when they do manifest. Later on in life I had a few as well, but they were mostly only flashes of situations or emotions which could be recognized when they came up later in daily life.

The experts also say that some people have them while they're awake, but the norm is while you're sleeping. Usually, the dreams have to do with dramatic or disastrous incidents. Sometimes they are exact photocopies, at other times they are vaguely the same or even symbolic. Yet, the dreamers all say they recognize these dreams as feeling different from normal dreams; that is why they take note of them.

Very often, people who dream of disasters try to warn the authorities about them before they occur, but one of the difficulties is usually, not knowing precisely when the catastrophe will take place. Another problem is being taken for a hoaxer.

What bothers me most is how the future can be seen in the present. I've thought about it and have come up with this idea: We know that our DNA runs on energy. Now, if dreams are energetic in nature, they may not necessarily be bound to the physical or the material. And therefore, may also *not be confined to time as measured on earth. We know about Einstein's theory on the relativity of time – the faster you move through space, the slower time moves, until it stands still at the speed of light, and then things change backwards again. So, it your thoughts aren't confined to your mind (look at Uri Geller) or by physical movement, it can do all the aerobics it wants to, as fast as it wants to. It can move forwards or backwards in time!*

Why, I wonder now, do I still have a hankering to travel? Can't my mind do it all on its own and come and tell me about it afterwards?

Chapter 15: Great kids

I read once that Walt Disney's granddaughter was positive that her grandfather was The Man who controlled rain, thunder and

lightning. During storms she would ask him to switch it off.

This innocence is often what makes children so funny.

We have a clump of trees at the bottom of our garden where the kids like to gather. I overheard the following conversation there:

Judy: 'My father can make blind people see.' (Judy's father is an optometrist.)

Bart: 'That's nothing. My mom drives the fastest car in the world. It's a Mercedes.' (The first time Bart made this claim Stephen wanted to know why I wouldn't buy a Mercedes. Not wanting to go into the mechanics of explaining why Bart's parents had more money than us, I said without thinking that I wouldn't buy a Mercedes – Ferraris were faster.)

Stephen answered the present challenge by saying smartly: 'It isn't. My mom says a Ferrari is faster and she should know. She sells the most panties in the world.'

If kids are so great, why can't we stop turning them into the asses we sometimes become? For instance: Cecil's mother wants to impress his more well-off school friends' parents on his birthday, so decides they can go with him to an expensive entertainment center. Cecil wants his best friend, Stephen, to go too, but either the budget or the friendship is under consideration, so Stephen is cut. Cecil's mom explains this away by saying that Stephen doesn't know the others.

Cecil wants to go to the entertainment center, so he goes along with the plan, but he feels guilty, as he went to Stephen's home grown party a few weeks before.

Stephen, of course, finds out about the party. He's hurt. He refuses to become enthusiastic about Cecil's birthday presents. The friendship is spoilt. That is not all – they both learn about manipulative behavior at a young age.

There's a 4 year old girl, Tina, who lives down the road. The kids in our street play together all the time, now in one's garden, now in another's.

Only Tina is not allowed to, because some of the children are a little older and her mom doesn't think it's safe. So, she remains at home, playing with her toys, being entertained by her mother, or watching television.

Stephen sometimes knocks on their door. They play, but it doesn't always end well. Tina throws tantrums when Stephen wants to leave. She wants to go with. Her mother smacks her legs when she refuses to calm down.

What can one say? Kids are great – a pity we make them grow up before their time.

Chapter 16: Broke again

    I don't know about you, but whenever I'm broke I get the urge to make something. Then all the scraps of material, the odd balls of wool and the leftover wooden planks come out. Turn nothing into something, so to speak. It makes me feel I'm

gaining something instead of going backwards.

Why I feel I have to gather when the bible says you should give away what you have I don't know. Half the time anyway, when things look up I shake my head and throw away the disasters I've made. (I hope it's nothing more than an insecurity problem – you tend to feel so unsafe when you run short.)

A car that's falling to pieces, threadbare clothes, and lack of money to buy more than the necessary foodstuffs; they all send me to the scrap cupboard faster than the cat can jump out of the window when Stephen chases her... He loves her really, he just can't stand it when she doesn't trust him – unfortunately she can't; he gets such mischievous urges.

More often than not though, being broke is quite good for one. I have a well-off friend who welcomes it. She finds it refreshing because it gives her a break from all the frivolous things she buys when she has bucks.

I think it spurs on the creative urge. Stephen,

for instance, is at the moment walking around in an aquamarine and cream mohair creation with sleeves up to his fingertips and a trunk that ends in the waistline. I put a crenellated pattern around the waist to make it look manlier. I did consider discarding it, as the wool is really meant for a feminine work of art, but I can't get it away from him, he says it's soft and warm. I can let him go through the winter like that, but it is rather worrying when so many neighbors kindly think of me when they want to discard their old clothes.

One has one's triumphs though. The cabbage casserole I made the day there was little else in the house had everyone licking their plates. Why didn't I write down the recipe? I know it took about half a shredded cabbage, onion and tomato, whole-wheat bread, salt, black pepper, garlic and tobasco sauce – but to get the ideal quantities...

When you need something which doesn't exist, you invent it. When something exists in the world, but you don't have or can't buy the real thing, you invent a make-do. A make-do can be a flop as often as not, but when it works, you're up there with the geniuses. One of our old Afrikaans

sayings is not for nothing: ''n Boer maak 'n plan.'
(A farmer makes a plan.)

Look at all those artists who enriched their art (and millions of people's lives through their poverty. How much worse off would the world not be without paintings such as Van Gogh's: The potato Eaters, or Max Beckmann's: Departure? Invention's mother may have been a deprived lady, but just look at her children!

Chapter 17: Enchantress

At first glance she was nothing unusual –
good features, medium build. She was the
receptionist at an engineering firm.

As she glanced at the catalogue, a regular client walked in. He was in his forties, quietly handsome, and his face took on a glow as he paused by the counter.

She was in her early twenties. Unlike most girls, or older women for that matter, she did not take out the G-string, wave it around, blush or giggle. She took out the most feminine camisole, as well as a lace two-piece. Calmly, she said she'd buy those.

While I wrote out the order, she and the client exchanged innocent pleasantries. By this time I was taking note: firstly because, before he'd walked in, she'd taken little note of the items she was now buying, and secondly, the man was wearing a gold band on his third finger.

Just then one of her bosses walked in, asking about an account. The client turned a shade redder, but the boss didn't seem to take any notice of him. He was smiling indulgently at the underwear. As he moved past her, his hand barely stroked her waist. (He was in his fifties.)

When he found what he'd been looking for, he had to pass close by her again. But this time he hesitated. The client murmured something like: 'I'll come back later.' The boss whispered in her ear as the other walked out: 'He likes you, Jane.' She replied as calmly as ever: 'Yes, he's asked me out to supper.' Nothing about whether she'd accepted or not.

10 days later, I was back with the delivery. Unfortunately there was no sign of the client this time, but both her bosses were working in the reception area. The other one was in his sixties.

While she was once again calmly looking for change, I noticed both men were watching her. Both looked as if they would dearly love to pay for the underwear. One's hand even moved to his pocket. Each had an unmistakable glow on his face.

Such a paragon needed more careful study: An olive complexion, loose brown curls to her shoulder blades, brown eyes with green flecks. (Take note: there was no seductive upward tilt to the eyes – too easy to associate with lust. These men were in love.) Her trouser suit was dark brown *off the peg, but fitted perfectly. She hardly wore any jewels, only one diamond ring on her middle finger. Her demeanor was quietly self-confident.*

What a female phenomenon! So underplayed that it most probably takes a man a while to notice her, but when he does he thinks he's discovered buried treasure. She knows how to lure them so they get stuck solid. And she certainly knows how to keep them guessing. What some of us learn at an early age!

Ah well, I may have to catch up on training, but one has to start somewhere. I'm off to the shops now to see what's available in dark brown.

Chapter 18: TV

My ex mother-in-law was fond of pastel shades. They went well with her white hair and blue eyes. She was also soft spoken. Her most vehement exclamation denoting reproof was: 'Oh dear.' What is amazing is that when she used her expression, you could feel dung clinging to you.

Yesterday I watched a television program about an uneducated man in need of money who became a terrorist. He killed quite a few people in a bloody, noisy way. When the killing started, I noticed Stephen frowning and getting that glint in his eye. I checked that the cat was out of the way, and sent him out to play. Then I switched the television off anyway. It was the violence formula again. 'Oh dear,' I sighed.

I decided to visit my neighbor. She was watching TV. Before I could complain she began explaining the story: The main character had been a poor boy that became an oil tycoon and married a model. He died in a plane crash so now she was rich, except that he wasn't really dead, but no-one's sure because now he's played by a different actor...Oh dear.

Perhaps the scriptwriters went on strike, I thought. A helpful suggestion to the producers might be to write up a contract with pulp fiction publishers, it would certainly be an improvement... but suddenly I got it; the whole aim of the romance formula was to get you into a zombie like state. The repetitive, drawn out nature of it is made that *way especially so that with tearful, glazed eyes or with envious, glazed eyes you begin to tape every episode in order to watch the rerun in bed. Addiction is the game.*

The intention with the blood, guts and gore formula is different. You're supposed to get jittery, and then foam at the mouth. If you can't convince yourself to clout someone you must at least shout at them.

Those are the intentions, but why television-,t and film producers who are guilty of this type of thing, don't realize that sometimes, just sometimes, by the time they've refined their winning formula, they should throw that formula in the dustbin – by that time the public is becoming nauseous from being force fed the same old story.

In real life, unfortunately, we have similar scripts. Come to think of it, that must be where unimaginative movie producers get their scripts from. Crime psychologists have come to the conclusion that 99% of crimes of passion are committed by highly sexed, dominant partners who aren't well educated and whose minds it has never crossed that you can learn to control your urges. It seems that in real life, violence and romance marry each other.

Premeditated murders are almost always committed for gain.

Political murders are usually committed under false pretences based on false information – and for gain, of course. Also, the opposite people get killed when the opposite party comes into power.

'O dear, oh dear, oh dear; you see where watching too much television gets you?

Chapter 19: Give me strength!

If by now you're dying to become a hawker,

let me give you some advice: *You cannot be timid. It can be put in another way: You can cure yourself of being timid, by becoming a hawker.*

When you're timid you are sweet to strangers, not because you like them, but because you fear them. Secretly you prefer animals; they don't say nasty things. They may think them, but they don't s... I just thought of our dog, Brownie. He does exactly that, without saying a word. On our walks he goes and sits in front of a garden gate where 3 dogs of various sizes live. I can see that he despises them, although he never opens his mouth, not once. When they hurtle themselves at the gate, sick with rage, he simply sits and watches them. After he has had his fill, he turns sideways and lifts his leg. After spraying the gate he will trot off, satisfied. Now if that's not painting a picture saying a thousand words, what is?

To get back; you also don't want people to buy from you because they feel sorry for you – sorry becomes discomfort after once and you want them to continue buying from you.

A friendly face is good, but for heaven's sake,

don't overdo it, you don't want prospective customers to feel sick. Besides, your true feelings are bound to erupt all over your family at the end of the day. And they're people you're usually not shy of at all.

Being timid is also the pits when a formerly enthusiastic customer wants to back out of a sales agreement. Shy people are afraid to give them hell, they tend to whine: 'But I've paid for these items you've ordered and what about my debts etc. This tactic usually evokes disdain, because face it; they really don't care about your problems.

If they've promised for another day and on that day payment is still not forthcoming, cut your losses, take a deep breath and start selling to other people. The first sale you make will heal the wound.

When your encounters are fleeting, you quickly learn to go for the necessary. You make the delivery date for the moment they've received their pay cheque. You give them your name and telephone number. You stress that if they want to cancel, they have to do it at least seven days in advance of delivery. Of course you've written down the style, size and color of their order, as well as their name and address. If possible, you pin their order to their telephone book, because they'll forget all about you the minute you walk out the door. After all, they didn't buy underwear from you; they bought a diversion from boring work.

Resign yourself that those who want to cancel won't phone you any time in advance. Usually, you'll find out that there's no money to pay for the goods when you arrive for delivery. (See, I told you I'll get to the drawbacks.) Here's a worst case scenario: A few women gather. They're not big earners, but are enthusiastic about what you have. Most of them order a little something. Something snaps in one of the women. She begins quietly by ordering panties for herself, as she doesn't want to be shown up in front of her friends for not buying. But since she's started she orders top and bottom sets for her little girls, underpants for the boy, ditto for the husband, and long johns for granny and G-strings for her sister. She even remembers that it will soon be winter, so she throws in a spencer for herself. A highly entertaining morning is had by all, you too, as the uppermost thought in your mind is that you've made your quota for the day – you can go home early!

On delivery day – payday – she says she's been so busy she hasn't had a chance to get to the bank, please come back Monday. On Monday you hear it's her day off. On Tuesday, if her co-workers are in the office, she pulls you into the passage and tells you all about the disasters and consequent unexpected expenses in her life, but don't expect she'd let you off the hook now – a family member gets paid on Friday, come back Monday.

Out of curiosity or a form of masochism, I'm not sure which, you can return until they begin to laugh at you behind your back. It certainly won't get you your payment.

No. What you do is this: When someone tries to make you invisible, you flip. You tell the person that they had their chance to cancel, but they didn't. If they don't have the money ready by the following morning, you're going to inform their boss immediately. (You both may know that he'll just tell you not to make your problem his problem, but she'll still be shown up in a bad light.)

Surprisingly, more often than not, she either digs deeper into her purse, or finds the necessary straight away, or she has it ready the next morning.

Take my advice; it will make the rest of the work quite enjoyable.

Chapter 20: Sexually speaking

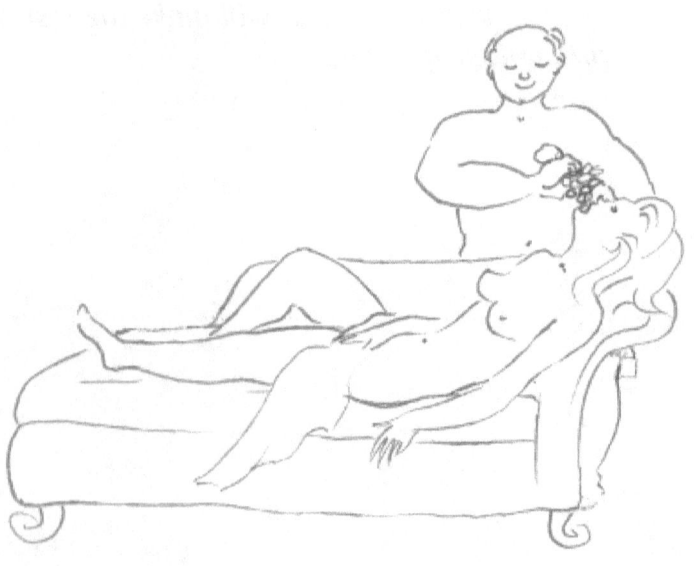

According to medical research, men reach a climax between 1-3 minutes after stimulation. Women take 8 minutes or more.

To me this seems like nature is looking for

trouble. How many innocent men must have wondered why their women were cold fish, and how many innocent women must've wondered why their men couldn't satisfy them, before modern technology explained things to us?

When women learnt to do a bit of running away to help her warm up, men got the idea that her 'No' always meant her 'Yes', instead of only sometimes. It's a bit like having a solid plate and a spiral plate on one stove.

Many men and many women have twigged, and respond appropriately to the above problem. But great confusion still reigns with the following: most men believe wholeheartedly that making love after a fight is a good way to clear the air. They feel that physical closeness will overcome the problem. This is really stoking the hornets' nest.

Women feel that after having fought with her, man still thinks it's OK to jump on her and violate her just to rub in his dominance. She hates it; it's a big turn-off, a lie against love. And when she acquiesces for the sake of peace, the chip on her shoulder grows to a boulder.

You see, underlying man's desire for physical closeness, is his dislike of analyzing emotional issues. On the other hand, woman loves dissecting emotional issues; she wants to understand perfectly and restore fully, before holding to her bosom – as stifling and boring as this may sound.

There is a third difference between men and women. Some men can have sex with a woman, not only without loving her, but while loving someone else... routinely. (Some people believe that your soul intermingles with intercourse and this is the route which leads to soul confusion.)

Nymphomaniacs may do this, but they have a medical condition. (Can there possibly be so many sick men walking around?) Normal women may do it for reasons like revenge, but not routinely, I believe. Usually she cannot separate sex and love. Her emotions are involved with the person she goes to bed with on a regular basis. If they are not, her interest soon fades. She will discontinue that relationship when she meets someone she can be emotionally involved with. Men seem to have the ability to separate love and sex. Rumor has it that they're surprised at western women being offended by the idea of a harem.

It has something to do with a woman's ego: For the man in her life to want to go to bed with someone else must make the competition more desirable, more attractive, and more needed – which in turn threatens her sense of security; her protector is leaving. The hunk who has the strength to kill the beast for food and fend off the dangers that beset her and the children wishes to keep the rain off another woman's head? Ha!

'Oi vey,' some women will moan, 'it's time for the beauty parlor and the plastic surgeon.'

In Saudi Arabia, of course, the rules are different, but the end result is the same. If your man is poor, you're the boss woman, if he's rich and has many wives; your ego is fed by having such a rich and powerful husband to brag about. Anyway, you're boss over every woman who comes after you – and he doesn't leave.

Perhaps nature's main reason for being so perverse in making the sexes so incompatibly different is to keep us on our toes. Otherwise, what would we do with our fighting instinct?

Chapter 21: Mom and the hospital

On Monday my mother said she was going to do the washing even though it looked like rain. She also reminded me to hand in the film she wanted developed to send to my brother.

Yesterday, that was Tuesday; she struggled through all the ironing and packed the slightly damp clothing in the cupboards. Who am I to complain about mildew? At her age Mom doesn't swerve off her regular path into unexplored territories. I simply took my clothes out of the cupboard again to air them.

Yesterday she also wrote to my brother, and then she carefully packed her overnight bag with everything on the hospital list. We almost had an argument about buying a toothbrush. She knew she wasn't going to use it. She always takes her teeth out and uses a nailbrush. But the list said to take a toothbrush, and Mom always follows rules.

She also phoned her eldest son, in case she didn't make it back.

This morning, she was up and dressed at 6

am. I could hear her walking around in her smart shoes with the low heels, which she'd polished yesterday. She made porridge and washed the dishes. Then she fell asleep in her chair.

At 12 o'clock, when I came back from work and picking up Stephen, Mom was pacing up and down outside. The hospital had phoned to say they had a bed for her. She was going to have a cataract removed from her right eye. Her left eye had been done some months previously.

My mom had explained to everyone that with her they didn't do the operation in just 10 minutes flat, as was the case with my aunt. She slept over. The first day they checked her heart as she suffered from angina as well as high blood sugar. (Here I have to explain that Mom is only slightly diabetic. She loves sweet things and eats as much sugar as she pleases – I've seen her finish off a small jar of ginger jam in a day. With half a tablet a day her blood sugar is normal, but on naughty days she has a full one.)

Stephen and I were just getting used to being on our own when Mom phoned from the hospital to come and pick her up. The doctor had said that as she'd forgotten to lay off the half a Disprin she takes every day, which thins her blood for her heart condition, she couldn't have the operation now. She was supposed to have stopped taking them already a week ago.

When I got to the hospital, mom was still in her pajamas. She wanted to have her supper first, she explained. Before we left she gave last minute advice to a nurse with man problems. Then she wished another good luck with a forthcoming exam. She was on first name terms with everyone. She wouldn't get dressed, she said while putting on her gown, so as to be ready for bed when we got home.

As we walked out of the hospital, I asked her whether she'd enjoyed herself. I'd just remembered that she'd forgotten to stop taking her Disprin with the first cataract operation as well.

'Oh, enormously,' said my mother. 'Of course, the staff treats you like a complete child. And if you play along it makes it so much more entertaining.'

Chapter 22: Cheap thrills

The bus was delayed by an accident. On the seat in front of me two old ladies entertained themselves by discussing the scene of the tragedy.

The slimmer one with the deep wrinkles and the dyed red hair said: 'Look at the tears on the little boy's face, Zelda. Shame, the mother has lost her shoe.'

Fat Zelda with the shiny dress said: 'The father looks deathly pale... I wonder if they're going to send for an ambulance.'

I looked at the victims of the accident. Of course a ten year old would cry – he's had a shock. His mother's shoe almost came off as she stepped onto the pavement, and the father didn't look shaken to me, he looked angry. The old ladies were just milking it for all they were worth.

The car wasn't even badly damaged. If only there had been a drop of blood; it would have made their day.

The accident reminded me of the time long ago, when ten of us girls went to see 'Love Story'. Being forewarned, the tissue supply was plentiful. Everyone cried so much the girls began asking for spares. I had to part with my bone dry ones. At the time I felt such a fool that I surreptitiously rubbed my eyes red so as not to be the odd one out. Today I realize that different buttons push different people's tear ducts.

Tragedy, love, beauty, drama; they all fill our eyes. Achievement is what makes me cry. The student who brought up six brothers and sisters, yet passed with honors. That man (I forget his name) who grew up in the slums of Paris, became a priest, built a hospital on an Hawaiian island with his own hands, then devoted the rest of his life to that community – he makes me cry. Even that old South African boxing champion, Gerry Coetzee, when he flung that lucky punch in the world fight, the one in which my excited sister-in-law jumped up to go to the loo for a 'wee' before the fight and when she got back the fight was over – he made me cry.

It was interesting to compare the impact the passing away of Mother Theresa and Princess Dianne had upon people. Both were well loved public figures who died within a week or so of each other.

Mother Theresa was of humble, Hungarian

origin. From the age of 18 till the day she died she dedicated her life to others. Her sole possessions were three changes of plain clothing. At around 40 she began schools in the slums of Calcutta by writing for the children with a stick in the sand. She started hospitals for the poor by begging for obsolete medicines from wealthier hospitals. She begged for ground, for buildings, for staff. By the time she died the nunneries of the little sisters who followed her example all over the world numbered 156. They say her beauty lay in the light in her eyes. Her spiritual strength was phenomenal. And these things really have me bawling.

Princess Dianne also had something to offer. Who's to say that providing the amount of glamour and charm she did weighed any less than the solid worth of Mother Theresa? Yet how many more women and even men watched the funeral service of the younger and I wonder for what reasons?

I also sometimes wonder about their dying so close to each other. Princess Dianne was a great admirer of Mother Theresa. Did they meet up in the afterlife?

Chapter 23: Spaceships

Scientific opinion is that we shouldn't dream of visiting outer space further than our own galaxy. We may be able to detect a star as far as a trillion light years away, but imagine how far away it really is if we could travel at the speed of light: 186,000 miles per second x how many seconds in a *year x a trillion.*

In our galaxy we have about a quarter percent chance of getting to a planet inhabited by intelligent life. Suns must burn consistently for long enough to engender life and planets orbiting the sun must be the correct distance away from it in order to sustain life.

The possibility of building spaceships that can travel at the speed of light does not seem to exist; as time slows down the faster you travel until it stands still at the speed of light. (That is where those science fiction stories come from of space travelers coming back to a different age.) Moreover, Mass is also a problem, as the faster something moves, the heavier it becomes, until its weight is infinite at the speed of light.

Scientists have posited methods whereby we could possibly move at about half the speed of light. They've also wondered about moving faster than the speed of light, whereby mathematically positive quantities become negative, but that is as far as the idea has gone.

On the other side of the coin; we've had

thousands of UFO sightings reported in only the last few decades.

They've been attributed to hoaxes, mistaken identities and hallucinations. But the more one reads about it, the more one realizes that these accounts are given by government officials, even presidents, professors, doctors, lawyers, anthropologists, teachers, television crews – all people with reputations at stake. Can they all be mistaken? Accounts which are documented for research are only those which have been vouchsafed for by witnesses. It is a subject which can too easily be torn apart.

The evidence we have is dubious, relying on witnesses and expert opinion. They are: Radiation in soil and foliage samples, indentations in the ground, photographs and film footage – the last never at close range.

In 1978 a film crew in New Zealand flew to Christchurch after repeated reports came in of UFO's in the area. When they spotted the UFO's they contacted air-traffic control in Wellington, who confirmed the sightings on radar. A light filled balloon shape emanating 5 pulsating lights was distinguished, which was filmed. This is the standard accepted report.

Incidentally, on radar they sometimes verify that the objects move much faster and in directions impossible for current human technology.

If we keep the vastness of infinity in mind, as well as the fact that the chances of intelligent life on other planets aren't zero, we have to accede that their development may just as well be as far in advance of us as backwards. Our development is certainly not going to stand still from now on, why should another's on another planet? We know that our sun is not the first, why should we be then?

Rumor has it that if we could find a wormhole, we might be able to slipstream past its tremendous gravitational pull into another galaxy in the wink of an eye! We'll look a bit further into electromagnetism and there you have it!

Chapter 24: Road to Oudtshoorn

You have to cross over the Outeniqua
Mountains to get to Oudtshoorn. I saw some
baboons on the mountain pass today. They more or
less disappeared while the construction company

was imploding for the wider thoroughfare.

After almost three years of getting over the mountain in stops and starts, we have smooth traffic flow, even with heavy duty vehicles on the road.

They have catered for all of nature's idiosyncrasies, such as rock falls and water flows. The low precipice walls were built from the imploded rock and indigenous flora was re-established. Look-out points with the odd picnic table have been set up. As Jane Austen would say: 'All is felicity.'

When you can put your car into fifth gear again, the road winds down to a basin surrounded by lower mountains. Here they mostly grow hops. Now, in springtime, the valley looks like it is covered in giant, silver cobwebs. These are the myriad of white vertical strings they attach to about 3 meter high wires on which the hop plants will clamber up.

After another 5 kilometers you turn left onto the Oudtshoorn road. Now it is hotter. The ground is more sparsely covered in low scrub; dark greens, grey and fawn. All along in between you find shades of pink flowering fynbos – Erica, Erigeron – one particular 2 meter tall shrub stands out. It has 3 centimeter big lantern like seed pods in shades from dark pink to cream. Today I found out what it is called. It is: 'Nymania Capenses' or commonly called Chinese Lanterns.

All along the road you are surrounded by hills. They are of a craggy rock strewn nature. One gets the feeling that you should be high up, but that the basin almost up to the road has filled up with soil.

Here and there, where a hillock has been cut through to make way for the road, it reveals a red earth full of rounded pebbles. Long ago there was an inland lake here.

In late Victorian times Oudtshoorn was an ostrich empire. Ostrich feathers were high fashion; women all over the world wore Oudtshoorn ostrich feathers. Its legacy is the upper class rock hewn houses with wrought iron trellis work. They all have covered verandahs against the hot summers;

some are wrap-around ones. As happens in hot, dry climates with cold winter nights, the people here seem closer to the earth.

We have a lot of rain in George during springtime. That is why it's good to come to Oudtshoorn's warmth at this time. In summer the heat can become unbearable. In winter again, it's colder than George.

In springtime, when you've completed the day's selling quota, you just begin to feel the heat. Then, the moment you enter the mountain pass again on your way back, the cool mists flow over you and through you. You feel rejuvenated, ready to seek the sun again tomorrow.

Chapter 25: Back to our roots

We returned to our roots when my mother and I moved from Johannesburg to George.

My great-grandfather lived in and was

swindled out of Oudtshoorn – at least, that is the story the family passed down. When everyone traded in ostrich feathers, he had donkeys. He couldn't read, so it was only after he'd swapped his span of donkeys for ostriches that he learnt of the collapse of the ostrich market.

As a child, my grandfather grew up near Mossel Bay, where his father had become a 'bywoner'. A bywoner works for the farmer in exchange for a house and a piece of land to cultivate.

My grandfather went to school for only a few months. After the Boer war, high Dutch made way for Afrikaans. In schools the English language was enforced. When my grandfather was caught speaking Afrikaans, a placard which read: 'I'm a donkey' was hung around his neck. This was too much for my great-grandfather. From that day on my grandfather was a shepherd who had to memorize verses from the bible every day for his education.

As a married man my grandfather lived in Great Brak River. Most people there, including him and his wife, worked for the Searles at their shoe factory. The land belonged to the Searles and the shops belonged to the Searles, so your rent and food bills were automatically subtracted from your pay packet every week. My mother told me once about a time during the great depression when grandfather came home on a Friday with only three pennies in his wallet. As soon as they could afford to, they moved to Johannesburg where wages were higher. Soon he made a down payment on a cottage on the outskirts of the city, in the area called Craighall Park.

In those days the city still had scope for growth, nowadays it is like an overripe pomegranate, spilling seeds unheeded. It is difficult to control an overgrown city; confusion and crime often reign and lawyers make a bundle.

At such a stage the inhabitants often yearn for something unspoilt, and the cycle starts all over again. Places like George, Mossel Bay and Knysna become draw cards – if you can make a living there!

My grandfather was happy for most of his

life in Johannesburg. His house sprawled out into a 5 bed-roomed Dutch Gabled place with many fruit trees and bee hives on his half acre stand (before he had to move them to a farm). He bought another stand in an area known as Linden, where history repeated itself. No-one informed him that when the area became a municipal suburb he had to pay taxes; when he tried to sell the property he was told that it had already been sold to defray said taxes!

It was a hard blow for my grandfather as it had clearly been intentional fraud – or so the lawyer informed him – but my grandfather did not have extra money and he was afraid to lose more in case his suit failed.

Such is life; while you try to get ahead you have to watch out for the wolves. Ironically, I am at the moment looking at a stand, a little further out of George... in Great Brak River in fact.

Chapter 26: Predictions

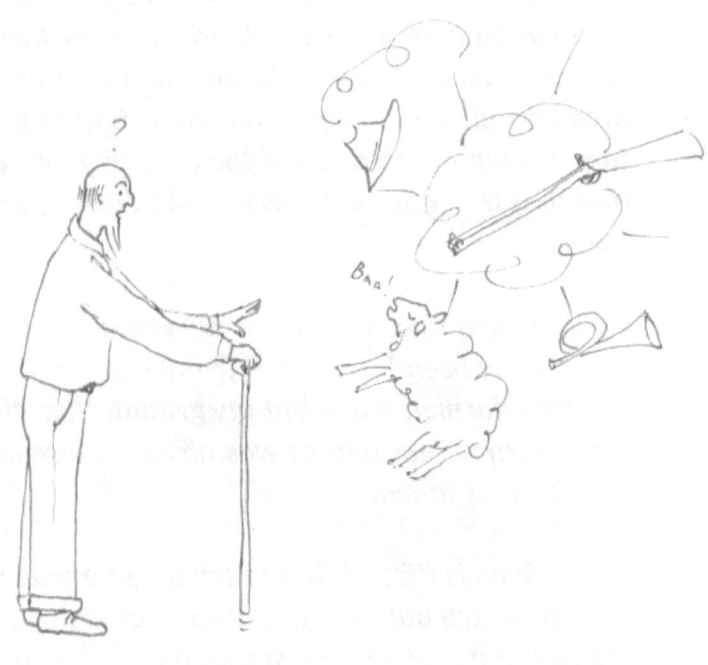

We South Africans also have our share of visionaries. Like Nostradamus, they have the uncanny ability of seeing into the future.

Our most famous visionary was an

unschooled farmer, a man they called prophet van Rensberg.

Like most farmers living in the Transvaal under the rule of Paul Kruger, he was deeply religious and deeply patriotic. He became famous locally when he foresaw many approaching dangers from the British forces during the Anglo Boer War. Now you know half the reason why we held out so long! The other half of the reason was most probably our pig-headed stubbornness in wanting to keep what was ours.

Prophet van Rensberg had visions on a daily basis. Some were about the next hour, some about the distant future. They appeared at any time in symbols, like those of Nostradamus. Also like the well-known visionary, his forecasts covered not only local events, but future happenings of the world. While he was alive he interpreted what he thought was significant, and his children kept a record of his visions, but after his death those who wrote about him interpreted his visions according to their own convictions.

His symbols, strangely, but in accord with

some other people who see things, were intrinsic to his own background. A 'voorlaaier' (an old style rifle which was loaded from the front of the barrel) would denote the Boer forces, clouds rolling in from the north would mean trouble from England, the world turning would mean time passing by and so forth.

Fascinating to us are his predictions about our era. Like some other visionaries he also foresaw 3 world wars. According to him the third would erupt suddenly between Asia and Europe, involving almost the entire world, but when over, peace would reign for a long time.

There was a Pope in the 11th century that was also well known for his visions. His version concentrated on the succession of Popes before the third world war, the bloodbath at the Vatican and the end of the Roman Catholic Church as we know it.

Nostradamus predicted a third world war in which the then Mesopotamia suddenly attacked Europe. St. Peter's Church would be destroyed. He also predicted worldwide co-operation after this war.

Other predictions of Van Rensberg saw the arrival of black leadership in South Africa, with the long standing Nationalist Party having a last foothold in the western Cape, before disappearing.

He foresaw the disappearance of Japan as an economic power and the emergence of South Africa as one, while America apparently decays.

Predictions in the past have been known to be inaccurate. They are also notorious for not being able to pinpoint time accurately. It may happen tomorrow, it may happen in fifty years' time.

So, what is the value of predictions? They seem to be warnings of imminent dangers as well as forecasts of probable futures. What can we do with this quirk of nature; take note and be prepared and when someone with this strange talent comes along when we're in the trouble zone, use him or her all we can – it may just get us through a war!

Chapter 27: Flying solo

All morning, while driving to Oudtshoorn, there've been pairs of birds flying overhead. A twosome of crows even cavorted in the middle of the road. Then suddenly there was this solitary duck flying purposefully south. You know how a duck flies; neck outstretched with wings laboring rhythmically to keep the rounded belly aloft.

Is there a pond somewhere with a mate waiting? What is south but the sea? Did something happen to its mate? Is this some kamikaze flight? It seems so alone while all the other birds are practicing pas de deux.

I cheer myself up by thinking that perhaps this is a young duck on his way to duck filled pastures. He is going to take female ducks by storm, as I am going to take underwear seekers by storm.

If he's lonesome, there isn't much left of my love-life either. Once in six weeks Stephen's father takes a duck flight south to combine pleasure with business. Which suits me well, apart from the bothersome feeling that such a situation could easily dry up to no love-life at all. And that is sad.

Marriage, I found after an immersion, needed resources I simply didn't have, at the time anyway. And let me tell you now; that story about Prince Charming picking you up on his white horse and riding off with you into the sunset... the person who first told it was an unmarried liar. Ignoramus!

Trite and naïve as it sounds, when I got married I thought that 'happily ever after' was automatic. The 50% of marriages that broke down were the ones where partners willfully and uncaringly stepped over invisible barriers. I, of course, belonged to the good lot – until I found myself one day sitting on the verandah wondering about the mess that had manifestly appeared on its own and declared it to be my marriage.

Then, after the divorce, another light glowed momentarily above my head: The man I'd been yearning for wasn't an angel either. (What did I expect, perfection?) He was Don Juan who preferred his women in harems. But, by that time I was tired of starting all over again. We became like a peanut butter sandwich; not as sticky as with syrup, but a little more wholesome. I even discovered that he liked his women to acquire a certain vintage...

After a while I stopped counting the women friends who've subtly and not so subtly conveyed to me what a fathead I am. I act all contrite, but I'm not really. As far as I'm concerned it's good for Stephen to get a glimpse of his father every now and then. So here's to the duck and here's to me!

Chapter 28: All that glitters

There are always a few crows on the road to Oudtshoorn. There are few road kills, so I like to think the crows are looking for shiny treasures by the road side.

And that reminds me of the innocence of children and what they deem to be treasures.

About six months ago we were treated to supper at a restaurant. The expensive meal didn't impress Stephen at all, but the plastic ruler advertising the restaurant and which we got with the bill, did.

He had a ruler at home, but the important factor was that now he had two. He spent a whole day deciding on the best place to store his two rulers. He didn't spend any time drawing lines with them. What he enjoyed most was to flick them, lick them, snap them... Strange. Even two weeks later he still asked where he'd last packed them away.

One of our neighbors the other day got him interested in putting a marathon effort in carrying bricks. She must have praised his strength – he's big on muscles lately.

Anyway, he came home with a pay packet, brown window envelope and all, with two, shiny silver colored coins. Boy was his face lit up. If he'd opened a chest of jewels he couldn't have been more wonder struck. I wasn't sure whether I should be ashamed at my previous stinginess, or proud of my son's joy at the realization that reward lay at the end of honest labour.

It's rather sad to see this innocence disappear so quickly. Stephen informed me the other day that I should buy a new car. Why? Because all his friends' parents have shiny, new, fast ones. Ours still gets us places, but it looks the worse for wear.

I think there's nothing wrong with having a lovely, red for instance, new car. It may be both an artificial and a superficial standard to judge by, but that is not the car's fault. Almost all of us find it difficult to grow up in this respect, whether we are Chinese and are aiming for the television set like the Wangs have, or American and negotiating for our own holiday home at the age of thirty. Personally, when I get jealous, I comfort myself by thinking that those who live in luxury must've borrowed the money or worse, and can't sleep at night.

There are few people who genuinely aren't

impressed with money – it is after all a yardstick by which to measure intelligent labour -apart from those who have so much they don't know what to do with it anyway. And with many of them it's again a case of financial challenges rather than finances that interest them.

I still wish I could be truly indifferent to material affluence, to be able to see past it all to something of value which makes material assets pale into insignificance. (Value is all around us, we just concentrate so hard on the one, that we lose sight of the other.) To people like this, money becomes nothing more than the shiny pieces of paper the crows collect on the side of the road.

Ancient Japanese poem:

There is really nothing you must be.

And there is nothing you must do.

There is really nothing you must have.

And there is nothing you must know.

There is really nothing you must become.

However. It helps to understand that fire burns,

And when it rains, the earth gets wet...

Chapter 29: Experts

'My dear child,' said my ex mother-in-law. 'That's not a gladiola. That's an Iris.'

'No,' said I, 'those are all Gladiolas.' I felt I should know. Wasn't I the one who'd for some months worked in a nursery? Wasn't I the one who was now doing landscaping work? (This was some years ago.) I felt obliged to stick to my guns. My ex mom-in-law felt she wasn't going to waste her breath arguing with a fool.

A week or so after her visit, I came across a photograph in my gardening book which clearly stated that my gladiolas were Irises. Needless to say I instantly became the fool she must have thought me to be.

About 2 years later, as an English trainer at a language school, I swore high and low to two fellow trainers that 'How are you?' in French was nothing other than 'Where are you going?' So adamant was I that the opposition gave in.

Imagine my shame when it came to me some weeks later that of course they were right. If a rubbish tip came and covered me at that moment I would have lain quite still without complaint.

Is it only I who suffer from these mind aberrations or does it happen to you too? Nothing sticks for long enough to be of lasting value. I have sometimes thought that if one stuck to one thing *for years instead of hopping around like a Jackrabbit you could end up becoming an expert. People who specialize in one thing their whole lives have my deepest admiration.*

During the language training phase I once had to interview a potential language trainee to assess his language skills. I got him to tell me about his life and work. Was I amazed to learn that he'd started off as a petrol pump attendant. He'd stayed with the company all his working life, but had moved up to become a trainer. At that stage he earned much more than I did, (we were more or less the same age) had a better home and a long standing marriage with children. I would never have been able to build up from his beginnings what he had.

On another level are the boys and girls who've hardly put on their adult clothes before they've made their mark. And my, do they ooze self-confidence!

An Olympic gold medal winner for swimming was interviewed on TV the other evening. She spoke with the type of wisdom that some of us twice her age cannot hope to attain.

'Oh, but all these public personalities are coached,' said a friend who does physiotherapy on them. That makes me feel only marginally better. They're still there because of a lot of determination. That kind of work one can respect.

By the looks of things, some of us are experts at life and some of us act like experts until we're proved the opposite.

Chapter 30: Smoking at the ears

You lose your patience or your temper. What happens? Your heart is over exited, your temples throb, and your ears pop, your jaw sets like a vice. Then your neck muscles begin to jam up.

Practicing self-control is to some extent a hit-and-miss operation. But let me tell you about a little miracle which, if it happened to me could happen to anyone.

Every now and then, in all lives and jobs, one has 'the irritant' popping up. The irritant can be your car, the plumbing or the computer, but usually it's dressed and eats and sleeps.

In underwear selling it's the woman who orders something, doesn't phone in time to cancel, then makes excuses on pay-up day.

You learn never to hand anything over until it has been paid for, but every now and then a slip-up occurs.

I won't go into how the slip-up happened this time, let's just say that (a month later) the day that payment could be hoped for again, started badly. After all, I'd had a month to fret already! My heart was racing and my ears were popping as I pressed the offending doorbell.

Anti-climax! There was to be no grand battle after all, not even a promise of later payment. After my fourth ring the neighbor peeked out of her door. She volunteered that the woman had moved – no forwarding address.

I shall gloss over my fury. Suffice it to say that an alarm bell rang at some stage, telling me to take a deep breath, and another, and another and so on. (As you can see, counting up to ten was not even in the running.) During this exercise, I tried to make my mind blank. Then the miracle happened. Taking so many deep breaths no doubt was the cause, but the high and the sense of peace that came with it was something to be experienced.

When I was once more myself it came to me: Blowing your top or driving around all day crying and cursing hurts who? You. Taking it out on someone else hurts them and you again when they retaliate. You can spoil your whole life walking around boiling all the time (and of course shorten it, but by that time you most probably wouldn't even care). Why give the silly old cow of an irritant the satisfaction?

It was just about 3 days later when the chance to practice my new skill came up. The irritant this time was the post office queue. I wasn't cross, just terribly impatient, so I didn't overdo it. Whilst breathing rhythmically, I did ponder about how much quicker things would progress if I did lose my cool – no quicker, in fact it would slow everything down. Then I began watching two people who were losing it. They were both tapping their feet, every now and then shifting their weight. They were fiddling with their fingers, sighing intermittently. The impatient man drew attention to himself when he got to the counter, by being rude. The assistant was short back to him. He developed red spots on his cheeks and it looked as if smoke was coming out of his nose; it was funny and I was so thankful it wasn't me!

Chapter 31: Noisy mom

My mother doesn't only need better eyesight; she also needs a hearing aid.

When she asks you anything and you reply in a normal voice, you can be sure her response will be: 'Hmm?' When you call out anything which requires an answer from another room the answer *is sure to be: 'What did you say?'*

When Mom calls us for a meal she makes it loud enough to be sure she can hear it as well. Result? All the neighbors think they've been invited for a meal too.

Although I've passed my fortieth birthday, my mother hasn't lost the habit of calling me Sissy. When there's a question mark after the name, she ends the second syllable on a high note. Can you imagine what it sounds like when she wants something and I'm out in the garden?

The difficulty is that Mom doesn't think she's deaf. I'm the one who mumbles – and the rest of the family and the radio and the TV. The TV ads are the only ones that don't mumble, when they're on it's only the vision which hasn't been tuned. The rest of the world behaves itself very well in my mother's eyes. Quietly.

We have a dam on the outskirts of George - a setting worthy of Switzerland. When we're there, even when some picnickers parked in a Combi behind us have Rock n' Roll music blaring from their loudspeakers, my mom has a beatific smile on her face. She'd sigh and say how peaceful it is out there.

But my mother does like Rock 'n Roll and she does believe in keeping up to date on worldly affairs, so she listens to the news every hour over the radio – in such a way that the neighbors can benefit too. She also loves to listen to her selection of old records. One day her mood may be for opera, another day it may be Boeremusiek and still another it may be her mother's old 78s. When she's transported, she'll sing along. On those days I quietly close all the windows and doors - if I happen to be home.

What I can't understand is that we haven't had any complaints yet. When I build a fire for a braai while the wind blows a bit, neighbours left and right close windows loudly to let me know I'm being obnoxious. So there's nothing wrong with their sense of smell. What happened to their hearing? Has my mother some special charm I don't have?

When I broach the subject of a hearing aid,

Mom counters that they cost too much. She also claims that she wouldn't be able to stand the noise the thing makes when it's not tuned properly. And the noise we all make. But if we can put up with all the noise she makes, why can't she put up with ours?

Chapter 32: Fascination

Here's one of nature's mysteries: a week or two ago the road to Oudtshoorn was suddenly covered with Sangolollos (Millipedes). Whichever way the road wound, there they were, all crossing

the road in a south-westerly direction. The following week there were some corpses and one or two live ones, moving back from where they had come, in line with north-east.

A sight which you always see on the Oudtshoorn road is the many ostrich feathers sticking to the scrub. Not the big white plumes, although you may see one if you're lucky, but the small, grey body feathers.

The other day I traveled behind a truck transporting ostriches. These small feathers were flying off at a rate of about one per second, making me wonder if the ostriches would be naked be the time we reached George. The ostriches were nervous, or curious, or simply trying to keep their balance, judging by the way they constantly moved their necks up, down, up and sideways. Their beautiful, long-lashed eyes were wide awake, assessing their situation.

Yesterday there was a lone one traveling in a bakkie. It had a sock with a cut off toe over its head. I wondered whether the sock was clean and if not, whether the ostrich minded.

Yesterday was a day for collecting overdue payments. The one customer I was nervous about, the other was a teaching advisor for special children, quite respectable, but she'd ordered big and was in danger of losing her job through affirmative action (giving black people vocational opportunities).

As it turned out, the advisory teacher's cheque was waiting, but the take-away place where the other woman worked was firmly locked when I got there.

I enquired next door. A well withered old lady, with the long, beautiful nails of a 20 year old princess, pursed her mouth disapprovingly: 'I'll eat my crown if you get your money,' she volunteered. Never-the-less, she explained the way to the run-away's house with many repetitions.

'By the station' she said, 'you cross the railway track which goes to Calitzdorp. You pass the bright pink, corrugated iron house on your left. Carry on until you come to the green house with the old stove, one of those Agas, in the garden. That's the house.'

I was so curious, I decided to go. When I got there, there wasn't only a stove in the garden; there were odd lengths of wood, three dogs and a fat little girl.

The first thing she said to me was: 'I'm playing in the church concert on Saturday night. I'm a fairy.'

Before she could elaborate on this interesting piece of information, a fat woman waddled out, carrying a broom. I recognized her as the daughter of the woman who'd placed the order.

Inside, the fatter mother asked me to excuse the mess. They'd entertained till late the night before, she explained. The lounge was actually extremely tidy, with many iridescent ornaments placed just so, the only reminders of the party mood. But there was a pervasive old dirt smell in the confined area. The focus point, hub, pride and mainstay, was the large TV.

The fat little girl had followed us in. She sat still, but was intermittently told to go and play outside. She interpreted the order as non-threatening, so ignored it.

The grown-ups happily opened up all the packets, inspected the XXXL panties, stretched the stretchy ones and discussed the quality. Then they regretfully returned them to me. There was a momentary brightening at the thought of an expected pension. I said that if they phoned me I'd come out again. On the way out I had to promise to try and come to the concert.

Overall it'd been a jolly occasion, I thought as I closed the gate behind me. The seat of my skirt was quite wet from something I'd been sitting on, and of course, the sale was only a fantasy in a few peoples' imaginations, but what price was that to pay when, for a while, you'd been kept utterly spellbound?

Chapter 33: Ou-nooi

The woman from down the road came to tell us that our Maltese had been run over. 'She was lying in the road – paralyzed', the neighbour breathed.

How pleased she looked at bringing the bad tidings, I thought. (She and her husband had been on at us about our dogs being in the street. After a while, in the spirit of good neighbourliness, I'd put wire mesh across the gates. Our other dog, Brownie, is a Toy-Pomeranian cross. They both used to squeeze through the bars.

Brownie, the Toy-Pom., immediately dug a hole underneath the gate. I had known he'd do it; it was just the speed of his reaction that surprised me. He's a stray who'd adopted us. He hates being confined to the extent that he can get over a 1.8m wall if it is face brick, like ours. Well, there went the breather I'd hoped my gesture would obtain.

The neighbour's husband was as self-righteous as his wife. For about a month he'd been driving out of his gate in the mornings, stopping his car by our gate, opening the gate to let our dogs back in, closing the gate and driving off. Our dogs, he had let us know, scared his wife to death by hurtling out to chase her car when she left for work in the mornings. I'm not completely heartless, I can see and sympathize with the problem, yet I wonder at the over zealousness of our dogs chasing her car – they hardly ever bother with other people's cars - and I shudder involuntarily when she tells us how much she loves our doggies and would hate to *crush them underneath her tyres.*

Anyway, as I hurried down the road I felt sure she was peeking through the curtain, thinking that we were getting our just deserts. I thought about my poor mother's eyes brimming over. Ou-nooi was her baby.

I saw Ou-nooi, not on the road, but lying quite still on the grass verge. Carefully, so as not to move her back or neck, I picked her up. She didn't seem to feel any pain. I shouted to my mother to open the back door of the car. We rushed off to the Vet.

The Vet manipulated her all over, declared nothing broken, gave her a sedative and a painkiller and said to bring her back if she didn't improve. I picked her up, this time with one hand under the breast. That was when I felt the speed at which her heart was pounding.

About 2 hours later Ou-nooi could sit up, but not move her hind legs. Then she began flopping her head backwards. Her eyes weren't looking at anything in particular; she simply hung her head back, then rotated it slowly.

Wait a minute; I thought as I ran to my mother's room. Sure enough, on the carpet, under the dressing table, were two small, white tablets. My mother's heart medication! No wonder the dog's heart was beating so wildly. Mine would too if I were her size and had had Ephedrine, painkillers and a sedative.

Ou-nooi stayed in wonderland for about three days. She'd never been a bright spark before, but from that day, it is sad to say, she hasn't been much more than a friendly cabbage on feet. Or so it seems to me.

I don't think our neighbour believed me when I told her the dog had not been run over. Since then they have moved. Our dogs have calmed down and no-one else ever complains. Thank heavens!

Chapter 34: Amongst grown-ups

With Stephen's father otherwise occupied in Johannesburg and us in George, I decided it was time to find a social life. More easily said than done!

My aunt suggested single's clubs. I told her

that all I could imagine of them was a bunch of women gathered on one side of a room eyeing a few men on the other side. Someone would put a record on (not a CD), the men would stake their claims and I'd be so petrified of being left wilting that I'd race out of the room, never to be seen again.

My mom suggested becoming involved in something I was interested in. One may just make friends who could introduce one to significant others. Ah, I thought - Pottery classes.

This is what happened; a term of pottery classes convinced me that you need the upper body strength of an ox to turn that piece of clay, and you were regarded as an outsider until your second year; seeming over eager puts women off and if you start your first day with a very bad nose cold you have made a lasting bad impression.

So, I joined the reading circle. They were very upper class. Once a month we got together at someone's home to discuss a book. Afterwards we had tea and cake. Competition was fierce as to who could produce the best tea and who had the most oriental rugs. As the circle was sizeable, no-one with a pokey home could offer to be hostess – not that upstart newcomers should dream of it anyway.

One hates admitting to a fault, but I have the one of, on meeting people, opening my mouth immediately and putting my foot in it. The reading circle was too well bred to ask me from under which rock I'd crawled out of and how soon I would return, please, so I persevered. Until one day a lady, who was quite conversant with the film version of 'Fried Green Tomatoes' but had not read the book, gave us a talk on the book. Somehow I never went back. Perhaps I shall again someday; the teas were always very good.

One day I saw an advertisement in the local newspaper: Walking tours for single parents and their children. Just the thing for Stephen and me, I thought.

The first one was a three hour walk in the Wilderness area. Each family had to take a picnic lunch; we ate at a rock pool where the children could swim. It was most pleasant. Stephen, who was only four years and some months, was very tired at the end, so the organizer carried him on his shoulders. He was a tanned, athletic looking man of 52. There were no other men present, only mothers and about 12 or 13 boys and girls.

About a week later this man phoned me up; and asked whether Stephen and I would like to go fishing with him. We went and both of us had a great time again. The man said that if I decided to have a braai at the new braai area I'd built and had been bragging about, he'd bring some fish along and show me some of his special recipes, which sounded good to me.

But at the braai things began to go wrong. He criticized my building methods and everyone knows one should never do that. Later on he told me smugly that at 41 I was actually much older than his usual girlfriends. When he said this he flashed his even white teeth. Before I could curb myself I flashed my slightly crooked white teeth and said that I usually went out with much younger men, in fact my current boyfriend was only 40. And that was the end of a beautiful friendship.

Chapter 35: Guardian angels

'I got a fine!' shouted my brother, 'and I knew it was going to happen, I felt it! About a block before the trap I felt I should slow down, but I thought I was being superstitious, so I didn't and there was the traffic cop with his hand up in the air.'

About a week later he came home with a big grin on his face: 'You know what happened to me today? He asked. 'I was driving too fast again. That little voice in my head warned me again, but this time I listened. And you know what, there was a speed trap again and this time they didn't pull me over!'

It happened to my brother a few years ago, but I thought of it again the other day when I was stopped by the traffic department. My problem had been tyres.

I say 'had been' because a week before this, while I was on my way to the bank to deposit the monthly bond repayment, I got a flat tyre. Disgruntled, I stopped at the tyre shop. It had been my third flat in three weeks. They were worn through to a shocking state. But when interest rates are high and money is tight, the banks must be smiling. In my frustration I took the bank's money to pay for two new front tyres, the best of the old ones went on the back. I knew it was time to replace the tyres, but I also had a strong premonition about being fined.

Three days later, out of the blue, I had an excellent selling day – the bank would get something after all. It was on my way back from Oudtshoorn that the traffic department stopped my car especially to check on tyres. When the officer warned me that I'd soon have to replace the ones at the back, I asked him what the current fine per tyre was. It was two thirds of a new tyre! I felt so thankful that I had not been fined, as there wouldn't have been a way that I would have been able to replace tyres on top of paying the fine.

Isn't it marvelous the way we are so often warned before impending disaster? Sometimes we're also warned about things we should do, or directions we should take in life. I once had a ticket to an opening celebration of a furniture store as I had just bought a video recorder. It is not the thing that one would normally bother about, but I dragged my mom and son along, as I felt certain that I was going to win something. (I'm not normally the type of person to win things.) I did. In the lucky draw I won a cleaning kit for VCRs, CDs and tapes. It may not sound like a fortune, but it was just what I needed and subsequently put to excellent use. It was also not a sure thing that I would have won something anyway; chances were about one in a hundred and prizes varied a lot in this lucky draw.

I wonder whether these are our own signals or whether such things as spirit guidance exist. When one reads up about it they certainly seem to. Or should one call them angels? Whatever or whoever they are, here's to them! There is nothing like the feeling that you're being looked after.

Chapter 36: Innocence

At the age of two he was adorable. And every year thereafter he became a little more capable, a

little sharper – alas, a little less innocent.

It's amazing how the brain develops. When I was being bowled over by my baby's large eyes, compact proportions and winning ways, the poor thing wasn't very bright yet. His attention span was so short that he lost interest in everything that wasn't under his nose. Even at the age of three he tried to hide his naughtiness by closing the door in my face while saying: 'We're not doing anything wrong.' You bet!

Unfortunately, by the age of five he's learnt to lie straight faced, even if the lies themselves are comparatively innocent. What a pity. I'd like to say it's all his little friends' fault, but can I really? I may as well say that it's their fault that I'm not as pretty or rich or perfect as he once thought me. Let me rather say then that it's because he's becoming a bright boy that he makes comparisons, examines critically and tests his boundaries. That doesn't mean that I don't miss the days when everyone and everything in his domain were automatically the best in his eyes.

Speaking of boundaries, five year old kids

also become hard of hearing, especially when an order is given in the vicinity of friends. Mothers are sometimes told they're being 'ugly' when they do some reprimanding. Luckily for us we're quickly forgiven and sought after for love and kisses. One hopes that with further growth the scales of resentment versus adoration stay balanced. Otherwise, how could parents with teenagers cope?

Pre-schoolers think they have the funniest jokes. This appreciation of the joke, you must understand, is a new thing. And what can be funnier than the 'No-no'? For instance, from the age of about two and a half, Stephen has been teasing the dogs and cats. Their annoyance makes the merriment all the greater.

Finally, a few months ago I thought the wheel was beginning to turn. Stephen was becoming fond of the cat. Whenever I saw him, he was stroking her. It was usual for him to be around the house, so I did not notice at first that this stroking went on where one or two grown-ups were also present. Strangely, it also made him giggle.

Eventually I discovered that the idea was not

to endear the cat, but to stroke her to such a degree of ecstasy that she'd open all valves. Her mouth would drool and she'd begin to fart. When she did it under someone's nose it was the height of entertainment.

What can one do with such a boy, apart from remembering the jokes that you thought were funny at that age – and hope the phase will soon pass?

Chapter 37: Mom has a new lease

Mom made a traditional Dutch outfit for my doll when I was ten years old. Originally, the doll had worn a wedding dress.

All her life my mother has been interested in

creative things – with a twist. Her Christmas trees might be bare branched and silver painted, her crochet work were 19th century collars (she has a marvelous encyclopedia of needlework which was written by a nun a century ago.) When she redecorated the lounge, the walls were papered in cream with a faint silver and gold willow pattern and all the cornices were gold a la Auntie Mame.

About five years ago Mom became ill and the doctors decided she needed a heart by-pass operation. She even went in to have it, but as usual came home without having had it. Her varicose veins weren't good transplant material, they said.

Mom had steeled herself for this operation. She'd been told that her life expectancy would be fifteen years more if she had it. When she came home operationless, she had to guard against this potential loss of life in some way.

Her decision for preserving her life was that she shouldn't do anything strenuous. She'd been frightened by doctor's jargon about lacerations of the heart muscles. Anything which tired her in the least should, in her opinion, not be tackled. In time, her mental list of what could and what couldn't be done adapted itself to what she liked and did not like doing. She liked to cook, so she was allowed to cook. Sweeping and dusting was not allowed unless the state of the house upset her heart. Embroidery was outlawed for a different reason; she could not see so well anymore.

The doctor told Mom that diabetics ate small meals more often during the day, so mom included snacking between her regular meals, with the obvious result. When we remonstrated with her, she said that all diabetics were fat, the disease caused it.

When mom and I prepared for the move down to George, things began to change, at first almost imperceptibly. A week or two before the move I almost thought she wasn't going to make it. She became quite ill, probably due to overexcitement.

We made it. At first a lot of building alterations had to be done, but as the house improved so did my mother's health. The altitude, the scenery, the stress free life, the new house and garden – all contributed to Mom's health. She discovered she could walk a bit further than just to the end of the block. She could sweep a floor if she put her mind to it and she could re-organize her books, given a little time.

Because she's short and rounded, Mom didn't want to buy herself a pair of slacks when we arrived (George dress code, as we can have 4 seasons in a day here). She called it a modern fad.

But when the Woolworth's sale came on, she couldn't resist just going to have a look. There she found a light-weight outfit in sage and orange which I couldn't get her to change out of once she began wearing it. We had to go back for another outfit.

This zest for all things new got her back to embroidering quite by chance. We found an unfinished linen tablecloth with embroidery cotton selling for the princely sum of 50 cents at a fête. We had more skeins of cotton at home. The cloth soon began to sprout flowers in all colours of the rainbow. It was quite original and rather lovely despite the fact that it was not as finely worked as *her previous efforts. Mom and I both could not stop admiring it.*

In her own way Mom is going full steam now. She has developed an itch behind one knee, which means she pulls up that trouser leg to scratch. Of course, she forgets to pull it down before going for her walk around the block, but that is a negligible consideration.

At this stage Mom is quite pleased she didn't have that operation. One or two of her acquaintances who've had it have not been doing as well as expected. I notice she's becoming fond of reading the obituary column now.

Chapter 38: Ghost on the stoep

The old lady in the material shop asked whether she could put her order on lay-by for a

while. She said that she'd had unexpected expenses.

Ninety-nine percent of the time when someone couldn't give a new delivery date it meant cancel. The previous time she'd ordered XXXL but hadn't taken most of her order as she said the items still looked small – so I hardened my heart. I explained that I was finishing off for Christmas and I'd paid the factory for her goods. That meant I'd sit with the expenses at least till February.

We sorted the problem out with a post-dated cheque. While she organized herself she told me what her expenses had been. She'd had to order funeral apparel as her son-in-law had died in a motor accident. (He had been one of six policemen on their way to a conference on stock theft when something went wrong with the vehicle. Sadly, three of them were killed, including her daughter's husband).

'You know,' she said, 'all last week I had cold shivers up and down my arms. My daughter even asked me what was wrong. I couldn't explain it, as I had no pain. And then this happened on Tuesday morning. It was as if I'd been waiting for it.

By this time I was feeling a cad about the money, so I stayed to chat for a while longer.

'This wasn't the first time something like this has happened to me,' she said, inviting me for a cup of tea at the same time.

'About 10 years ago I came out onto the verandah one evening. The streetlight was shining partly onto it. It was stuffy in the house and I needed a breath of fresh air. My husband hadn't been well for some time, although he still got around in a wheel-chair. He remained in the house.

I'd been outside for a little while when I sensed that someone else was on the stoep. He was standing a few feet away from me, obscured by the shadows, but I could feel him looking at me. He was dressed in the same way my husband usually dressed, with his hat on.

I wasn't afraid, just uncertain, and then suddenly the thought crossed my mind that I should go inside. When I got to my husband I discovered that he'd passed away during the time I'd been outside.'

'There's obviously more to life than meets the eye,' she continued, 'I sometimes think we're a bit dense as to what life is all about.'

I said: 'Well, they say we only use about 10% of our brain's capabilities, perhaps the other 90% is will catch up when we understand what spiritual life is all about.'

The old lady sighed, then said: 'It's as if they're trying to let us know that another life is out there, but they can say no more.'

She made an effort to cheer up: 'Well dearie,' she said while collecting my tea cup, 'there's a time for everything and it looks like I'll be here for another Christmas.' She heaved herself up and waddled off towards the back, waving her hand at me.

Chapter 39: Christmas stocking

'The toilet sounds just like little cars running around on the carpet,' says my sleepy son.

Straining my imagination, I think: Perhaps steam powered ones.

I'm disappointed that he didn't mention bicycles. I brought one back from Oudtshoorn this morning. He had a peek when I put it away in the cupboard till Christmas, but so far he's very quiet about it. Perhaps he feels unsure as his neighbourhood friends have been riding for over a year and he doesn't know how to yet. Perhaps he thinks the bike is a reject, because of its odd colored accessories. I think they look charming, besides, it was a bargain because of them.

Today was also, gloriously, the last delivery day of the year. Wonder upon wonder only one person cancelled.

This year I rounded things up early. The house has been rented out to holiday-makers, so there is a lot of spring-cleaning to be done. We're moving into a room in the back garden for the duration. Just like camping, I'm trying to impress on Stephen, as we are going to rough it on foam mattresses. My mom is going to my brother's farm for most of the time.

'Mommy?' Stephen interrupts my thought flow: 'I don't think I'd like marbles in my Christmas stocking after all.'

'No,' I mutter, 'Granny will only slip on them.'

'I'd like a packet of marshmallow ice-cream cones with hundreds and thousands on them.'

Although my opinion of them is that they're hideously unhealthy I don't veto the idea. Tomorrow it will be something else. Unlike the bicycle, the amount of pleasure he's had up till now out of this as yet nonexistent Christmas stocking, far outweighs the pleasure he'll get out of the real thing. And we still have 24 days to go!

'Mommy? What do animals that live in the veld get for Christmas?'

I think for a moment. 'I know what I wish

the farmers would get their animals for Christmas.'

'What?'

'Every time, on a hot summer's day, when I drive past farms with animals – I even saw a bunch of turkeys like this once – and they have no shade, I wish the farmer would get them a shade tree. One that is drought resistant, like the Australian Pepper tree. An indigenous one may be better,' I add guiltily, 'but I love the Willowy feel of the Pepper tree.'

'I wish it too,' says my sleepy son, 'then they won't get any more headaches.' He falls asleep.

I stay awake a little while longer, planning on how to teach him a little how to ride at the park before his friends see him. He may be worrying about them teasing him if he can't balance on his bike.

Then I begin to fantasize about what I would like for Christmas:

Christmas stockings for middle-aged women

Should be filled with;

A good man in their lives,

Some lady friends,

Children who love them,

Parents who are healthy and hearty,

And someone else to make Christmas dinner

Chapter 40: Paw-paw

'I think this paw-paw you bought is still green,' says my mother.

She's sitting in her own easy chair again. The holiday-makers have gone and for the past week it's been difficult to get her out of it.

I don't take much notice. My underwear

catalogue is in a dreadful state. That wouldn't do for Knysna. Knysna, the tourist attraction of the area is too status conscious to tolerate tatty catalogues.

There is a double hi-way from George to Knysna. Your views are of lakes, tree plantations, holiday homes and the sea at Wilderness. Where the road to Oudtshoorn is narrow and the environment harsh, here all around you is comfort and greenery.

Knysna is geared for tourism. In its shops you can be amazed, delighted and charmed by the array of the latest nick-knacks. One wonders at the ingenuity of the people who dream them up.

Many people also think it's hard to keep up with high rentals as well as the high tourist geared cost of living. The only other thing that Knysna is big in is indigenous wood; Stinkwood, Yellow-wood, Blackwood – when you walk into one of their factories you itch to buy.

Because generally speaking prices are high in Knysna, my prices compete well. It's worth it to have a good display.

'Mommy, I also want some paw-paw,' says Stephen.

'Don't interrupt Mommy,' says my mother, 'I'll get you some.'

Stephen gets his paw-paw but spits out the first mouthful. 'This isn't paw-paw,' he shouts. 'It's hard!'

This gets my attention. 'If it's the paw-paw I bought last week, perhaps it's old.' How can paw-paw be hard? What's that crunching sound? You don't crunch paw-paw. I get up and walk over to where my mother is crunching away, unperturbed.

'Mother dear,' I say when I see what she's eating, 'this isn't paw-paw. It's the half a pumpkin I bought this morning,' (a Boerpampoen with an orange skin.)

'Of course!' says my mother, jumping up, I thought it tasted strange. It was just the sugar and lemon that confused me... and why did you have to

*buy one with such an orange skin? It's confusing!'
she takes Stephen's plate and hurries back to the
kitchen. What can I do but shake my head.*

*'You know,' she says after a while. 'This
cataract operation hasn't worked that well,
otherwise I would never have mistaken pumpkin
for paw-paw.'*

*'It's not the operation, Mom. You're wearing
your old glasses again. The doctor told you that
your prescription will be different now. We have to
get you new ones.'*

*'Doctors,' mutters Mom. 'What do they
know?' They tell you that you need operations
when you don't, and they tell you that you don't
need pills when you do.'*

*I don't answer. I am simply content that
things are back to normal in our household.*

Other titles by Estelle Hough

Manage your Life Book 1 covers how your brain thinks and how to train it.

Part 1: How your brain thinks

Chapter 1: The way life works
Chapter 2: The way our brains work
Chapter 3: Mistakes we make
Chapter 4: Creative thinking
Chapter 5: Taxing the conscious brain
Chapter 6: Correcting areas of dysfunction

Part 2: How to heal your brain

Chapter 7: Fear, panic, stress, and anxiety
(basal ganglia) and what to do
Chapter 8: Depression
(deep limbic system)
Chapter 9: Banishing depression
Chapter 10: Worry and obsessiveness
(cingulate system) and what to do
Chapter 11: Memory and temper
(temporal lobes) and what to do
Chapter 12: Attention deficit disorder
(pre-frontal lobes) and what to do

MANAGE
YOUR LIFE

BOOK 2

HUMAN CONCERNS
AND
GROWING PSYCHOLOGICALLY

ESTELLE HOUGH

Manage your Life Book 2 covers common concerns people have. It also covers growing psychologically.

Common concerns:

Chapter 1: Obesity, anorexia nervosa, bulimia, gaming
addiction
Chapter 2: Impact of drugs and alcohol on the brain
Chapter 3: Jealousy, obsessiveness
Chapter 4: Cognitive restructuring to cure bad habits
Chapter 5: Coping with long term mental challenges

Growing psychologically:

Chapter 6: Understanding people
Chapter 7: Self- esteem
Chapter 8: Self-confidence
Chapter 9: Interactions with others
Chapter 10: Communication
Chapter 11: Romance, marriage and love
Chapter 12: Children

Manage your Life Book 3 covers acquiring mental skills and getting the most out of life.

Part 1 - Acquiring skills

Chapter 1: Managing life and becoming happy
Chapter 2: Skills of value
Chapter 3: Enthusiasm and goals
Chapter 4: An overview on happiness
Chapter 5: Achieving balanced success
Chapter 6: Affirmations, visualizations

Part 2 – Surfing life

Barry and the old folks

Barry finds clues to a lost inheritance

belonging to his grandfather and two aunts - but there are villains who have been searching for the same treasure since the time when the diamond mine of Kolmanskop in Namibia was in operation in the 1920s.

Complete guide to getting your house built

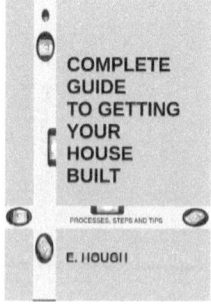

This booklet takes you through all the processes, steps and tips of house building

www.ingramcontent.com/pod-product-compliance
Lightning Source LLC
Chambersburg PA
CBHW020438180626
46812CB00003B/1302

9780620626668